Praise for
All the Earth, Thrown to the Sky

"While there's plenty of Dust Bowl period atmosphere, this is at heart a classic road-trip tale, laced with danger and an unexpected (but welcome) sprinkling of humor."
—*The Bulletin*

"A fast-paced, exciting story in which historical details are smoothly incorporated, characters are quickly but effectively sketched, and the author's Twain-like twang delivers both ironic and situational humor that will leave readers chuckling."
—*SLJ*

"A solid yarn with just a hint of romance."
—*Kirkus Reviews*

"A well-paced adventure [with] three exceedingly likable misfit characters."
—CityBookReview.com

"Lansdale has captured the spirit and fortitude of the young orphans who survived the Great Depression without a support system. . . . Readers will find the exploits of Jack, Jane, and Tony entertaining and informative. The book would be a great tie-in to a study on the Great Depression."
—*VOYA*

All the Earth,
Thrown to the Sky

All the Earth, Thrown to the Sky

JOE R. LANSDALE

EMBER

Text copyright © 2011 by Joe R. Lansdale
Cover photograph copyright © 2011 by Emmanuelle Brisson/Getty Images

All rights reserved. Published in the United States by Ember, an imprint of
Random House Children's Books, a division of Random House, Inc., New York.
Originally published in hardcover in the United States by Delacorte Press,
an imprint of Random House Children's Books, New York, in 2011.

Ember and the E colophon are registered trademarks of Random House, Inc.

Visit us on the Web! randomhouse.com/teens

Educators and librarians, for a variety of teaching tools, visit us at randomhouse.com/teachers

The Library of Congress has cataloged the hardcover edition of this work as follows:
Lansdale, Joe R.
All the earth, thrown to the sky / by Joe R. Lansdale. — 1st ed.
p. cm.
Summary: When the devastation wrought by endless dust storms in 1930s Oklahoma makes orphans of Jack, his schoolmate Jane, and her brother Tony, they take the truck of a dead man and set out to find a new start.
ISBN 978-0-385-73931-3 (hc) — ISBN 978-0-385-90782-8 (lib. bdg.) — ISBN 978-0-375-89748-1 (ebook)
1. Dust Bowl Era, 1931–1939—Juvenile fiction. [1. Dust Bowl Era, 1931–1939—Fiction. 2. Automobile travel—Fiction. 3. Orphans—Fiction. 4. Brothers and sisters—Fiction. 5. Depressions—1929—Fiction. 6. Oklahoma—History—20th century—Fiction. 7. Texas—History—20th century—Fiction.] I. Title.
PZ7.L2795All 2011
[Fic]—dc22
2010029260

ISBN 978-0-385-73932-0 (tr. pbk.)

RL: 5.5

Printed in the United States of America

10 9 8 7 6 5 4 3 2 1

First Ember Edition 2012

Random House Children's Books supports the First Amendment
and celebrates the right to read.

To Bud and O'Reta Lansdale.
They survived the Great Depression,
and their memories of that time inspired
many of the stories I've written,
including this one.

Thanks to Stephanie Elliott, my editor;
Krista Vitola, her assistant; and Danny Baror,
my agent, for their time and help.

1

The wind could blow down a full-grown man, but it was the dust that was the worst. If the dust was red, I could figure it was out of Oklahoma, where we were. But if it was white, it was part of Texas come to fall on us, and if it was darker, it was probably peppering down from Kansas or Nebraska.

Mama always claimed you could see the face of the devil in them sandstorms, you looked hard enough. I don't know about that, it being the devil and all. But I can tell you for sure there were times when the sand seemed to have shape, and I thought maybe I could see a face in it, and it was a mean face, and it was a face that had come to puff up and blow us away.

It might as well have been the devil, though. In a way, it had blowed Mama and Daddy away, 'cause one night, all the dust in her lungs—the dirty pneumonia, the doctor had called it—finally clogged up good and she couldn't breathe and there wasn't a thing we could do about it. Before morning she was dead. I finally fell asleep in a chair by her bed holding her cold hand, listening to the wind outside.

When I went to look for Daddy, I found him out in the barn. He'd hung himself from a rafter with a plowline from the old mule harness. He had a note pinned to his shirt that said: I CAN NOT TAKE IT WITH YOUR MAMA DEAD I LOVE YOU AND I AM SORRY. It was not a long note, but it was clear, and even without the note, I'd have got the message.

It hadn't been long since he done it, because there was still a slight swing to his body and his shadow waved back and forth across the floor and his body was still warm.

I got up on the old milking stool and cut him down with my pocketknife, my hand trembling all the while I done it. I went inside and got Mama, managed to carry her down the porch and lay her on an old tarp and tug her out to the barn. Then the sandstorm came again, like it was just waiting on me to get inside. It was slamming the boards on the outside of the barn all the time I dug. The sky turned dark as the inside of a cow even though it was midday. I lit a lantern and dug by that light. The floor of the barn was dirt and it was packed down hard and tight from when we still had animals walking around on it.

I had to work pretty hard at digging until the ground got cracked and I was down a few inches. Then it was soft earth, and I was able to dig quicker. Digging was all I let myself think about, because if I stopped to think about how the only family I had was going down into a hole, I don't know I could have done it.

I wrapped Mama and Daddy in the tarp and dragged them into the hole, side by side, gentle as I could. I started covering them up, but all of a sudden, I was as weak as a newborn kitten. I sat down on the side of the grave and looked at their shapes under the tarp. I can't tell you how empty I felt. I even thought about taking that plowline and doing to myself what Daddy had done.

But I didn't want to be like that. I wanted to be like the heroes in books I had read about, who could stand up against anything and keep on coming. I hated to say it about my Daddy, but he had taken the coward's way out, and I hadn't never been no coward and wasn't about to start. Still, I broke down and started crying, and I couldn't stop, though there didn't seem to be much wet in me. The world was dry, and so was I, and all the time I cried I heaved, like someone sick with nothing left inside to throw up.

The storm howled and rattled the boards in the barn. The sand drifted through the cracks and filled the air like a fine powder and the powder was the color of blood. It was Oklahoma soil that was killing us that day, and not no other. In an odd way I found that worse. It seemed more personal than dirt from Texas, Kansas, or the wilds of Nebraska.

The lantern light made the powder gleam. I sat there and stared at the blood-colored mist and finally got up the strength to stand and finish covering Mama and Daddy, mashing the dirt down tight and flat with the back of the shovel when I was done.

I started to say some words over them, but the truth was I

wasn't feeling all that religious right then, so I didn't say nothing but "I love you two. But you shouldn't have gone and killed yourself, Daddy. That wasn't any kind of way to do."

I got the lantern and set it by the door, pulled some goggles off a nail and slipped them on. They had belonged to my granddaddy, who had been an aviator in World War I, and though I hadn't knowed him very well before he died, he had left them to me, and it was a good thing, 'cause I knowed a couple fellas that got their eyes scraped off by blowing sand and gone plumb blind.

I put the goggles on, blew out the lantern. Wasn't no use trying to carry it out there in the dark, 'cause the wind would blow it out. I set it down on the floor again, opened up the barn door, got hold of the rope Daddy had tied to a nail outside, and followed it through the dark with the wind blowing that sand and it scraping me like the dry tongue of a cat. I followed it over to where it was tied to the porch of the house, and then when I let go of it, I had to feel my way around until I got hold of the doorknob and pushed myself inside.

I remember thinking right then that things couldn't get no worse.

But I was wrong.

2

There was plenty of rabbits for a while, so many that the men and boys would go out in groups and run after them and chase them up against some makeshift fences like they was cattle, then take sticks to them and beat them to death. There was so many rabbits they were eating everything green that the starving livestock and the grasshoppers hadn't eaten and the sand and the drought hadn't killed. Some of that green was our gardens. We didn't want to give it up to rabbits, and on account of that, the rabbits was herded and killed.

Food wasn't all that handy, so me and Daddy, after killing some rabbits, used to get us a bunch of them and bring them home to eat. We'd got some a couple days back and hung them in the house on a nail. After Mama got worse sick we'd forgot about the rabbits and hadn't eaten for two days. Now, with Mama and Daddy dead and no one left but me, they'd gone hard and were beginning to smell a little ripe. I decided I was going to skin them, cook them, and eat until I couldn't eat no more.

The sand was still blowing, and it was coming through the house the way a ghost would walk through a wall. We had got some flour and water and made some paste and glued paper all along the edges of the windows with it, and we put rags up against the door once we got inside, but it didn't help much. The dust still got in. It was everywhere. In the curtains and on the shelves and in the pages of books, and it coated the face and tipped the tongue and gave everything you ate a trail-spice taste. I was always wiping or washing it out of my eyes.

I had buckets of water pumped up from our well in the barn, it was the one good thing about our place. All the other wells was dry or near dry, but ours kept pumping. The barn kept the sand from blowing in as bad as it might, so our well hadn't dried up like so many others.

I had put a rag over the water buckets, and the top of the rag was dark with dust. I got the dipper and shook the dust off it and lifted off the rag and dipped me a drink and put the rag back. The water tasted like I was dipping it out of a mud puddle. Rag or not, the dust had got in.

I cut up the rabbits and tossed the innards in an empty bucket. I had been giving things like that to our dog, Butch, but the dog couldn't stand the sand neither, and one day he went off and didn't come back. I liked to imagine he had gone out to California and was living under a tree in an orange grove and there were kind folks who gave him food. California was a place some said everyone ought to go. Said there was work there and there wasn't no sandstorms and there was plenty of water that didn't taste like grit. After all that had happened, I was thinking on it. It wasn't like I had a lot to pack. And besides, the bank was going to take back the property any day now.

I cleaned the rabbits and put some sticks of wood in the stove and lit them and fried the rabbits with a little lard and flour. I didn't have any eggs, so the batter was flakey and mostly fell off.

I ate some of the meat and put the rest in the icebox, which didn't have any ice but was about as good a place as there was to keep the dust out. I kept thinking about those rabbits, us killing them and them screaming the way they do, like dying women in lakes of fire is the best I can describe it, but truth to tell, there ain't no words for it. If I thought too much on it, it spoiled my eating, so I tried to think pleasant thoughts, but right then I didn't have many.

I took some time to step on centipedes, which were all over the place, and I killed a scorpion that was under the table the same way. I didn't want to lay down and have those things on me. When I was younger, a scorpion had stung me, and I didn't like it a bit and didn't want to repeat it.

When I had killed all I could see, I went over and lay down on the bed where Mama had died. I could smell her on the mattress, the kind of sweet smell she had that didn't have nothing to do with perfume, 'cause she didn't have any except once a bit of lilac water and it was long gone. It was just Mama's smell and it made me cry. I cried and cried and finally I went to sleep.

Outside it was still dark and the sand still blew.

3

I dreamed and remembered how things had been before all the sand. It was a memory thin as the film covering an egg yolk, but it was a memory I liked. I thought about when Mama and Daddy had been happy. How I had been happy too. We hadn't had much, but there was food to eat and time to be together. They talked about the future like there would be one. They did good honest work, and I went to school and did chores, and when we could, we listened to the radio or talked or sang or laughed. Me and Daddy played checkers while Mama washed the dishes. It wasn't a big life, but it was a good life.

And then the soil got dry and the plants went dead. Wasn't nothing to feed the stock, and the only thing left to do was eat them, not only so they wouldn't starve to death, but so we wouldn't either. We even ate the horse, which turned out to be a little stringy and sweet, so under normal circumstances, I don't recommend it. Right then, though, I would have eaten horse or dog or most anything. There came a point when it seemed like I was hungry all the time.

After the crops started to fail from it being so dry, the wind came and plucked them up and finished them off. The wind howled like a wolf, and it was full of sand that scraped and chewed and cut down everything in its path. When the wind wasn't blowing, the starving grasshoppers was coming at us in a wave so dark it blacked out the sun. And the rabbits. So many rabbits. Everything became a big mess of whirling sand, starving rabbits, and buzzing grasshoppers.

Then the memory of that faded, and all I could see was that grave in the barn. Open, with Mama and Daddy wrapped up in it. I was standing over it, looking down. A hand pushed up from inside the tarp, pushed at it so that I could see its shape. It was a small hand. It was Mama's hand.

I come awake quick, tears running down my face.

The dark was gone and so was the sandstorm. I sat up and listened to make sure, but didn't hear any wind. Still, the air was full of fine powder.

I got out of bed and went out on the front porch and pushed three inches of dust off the path from the door to the steps with my shoe. Then I scraped the steps clean. The air was still and the sun was high and the sand had changed the way everything looked again. The earth was Oklahoma red, where yesterday it had been Texas white with some Nebraska black thrown in for good measure.

There were big dunes of sand all over the place, and I could see in the distance that the storm had knocked down what was left of our barbwire fence. It didn't matter. All the cows that had been inside it were long dead anyway.

And then I seen her and him trudging across the sand. She was wearing boots and dungarees and a plaid shirt buttoned close to the neck and at the wrists to keep the dust out. The boy with her was younger than her, and he had on worn overalls and an old brown shirt. They was both carrying flour sacks stuffed full of something.

They was coming along slowly, and I could see they didn't have no real strength left and was about to fall over, so I started out to meet them. My feet bogged in the sand as I went, and it took me a while to get up to her, and when I was close, I seen the girl drop to one knee. Now that I could see her good I knowed her right off. It was Jane Lewis, which meant the kid was her little brother, Tony. I hadn't seen them in ages. Mainly because they was known to have lice on a regular basis, which was an affliction of many in the area. I'd had them myself from time to time. Mama, however, had come to the idea that the Lewises were lice-ridden by nature, so I wasn't allowed what she had called "an association" with them.

Lice or no lice, I went over and got an arm under Jane, helped her up, and took the flour sack from her. It was as heavy as if it was packed with stones.

I said, "It's me, Jane. Jack Catcher."

"I know that," she said.

"Well, all right," I said.

I helped her toward the house, and Tony came stumbling after. He said, "You know me, don't you?"

"You're Tony," I said. "I know her, I'm bound to know you."

"I can't see so good," he said. "The sand burned my eyes."

"Can you see to grab onto me?"

He came over and took hold of my shirttail. I helped Jane to the house, and Tony clung to me until we was up the steps and on the porch. Inside, they collapsed on the floor. Jane unwrapped her face and shook her head, snapping sand across the room. When she was through doing that, her dark brown hair fell down to her shoulders, and even dirty as she was, I noted she looked pretty good, though I took into consideration her family's reputation and watched for lice.

I got a rag that wasn't as gritty as some of the others and shook it out. I got some water from a bucket and soaked it a little. I took it over to Tony and pulled the covering off his face and wiped him down with it. When I got through wiping, I saw that what I had thought was tan from the sun was brown from the dirt. Underneath it all, he was as white as the belly of a fish. He had a bony face and his hair looked like a rained-on haystack with chicken manure in it, the way it was stuck together in spots.

"I still can't see none," he said, lightly rubbing his eyes.

I helped him up and led him over to the bucket and used the dipper to pour water directly into his eyes. He blinked while I done it, but mostly managed to keep his eyes open.

"That's better," he said. "You don't look like you're made of sand now. Everything I been looking at looked sandy."

"Good," I said, "'cause I feel like I'm made of sand."

They drank some water then, and I got some of the rabbit out of the icebox and put it on the table. They sat and ate. When Jane had her piece of rabbit down to the bones, she said, "That tasted a little gritty and right near spoiled."

"Well," I said, "I'll tell your waiter to tell the chef, and the chef will tell you to go to hell."

She looked at me and drooped the corners of her mouth. "I didn't mean it like that. I was just making a comment."

"Yeah, well," I said, "I don't reckon you been eating all that much that ain't gritty, sister."

"And you would be correct," she said. "I apologize."

"But it didn't taste so good," Tony said.

"That's 'cause it was a rabbit that had been dead awhile," I said. "I cooked it hard on account of that. I guess now you'd like dessert and some finger bowls."

"That would be nice," Jane said, "and maybe a nice hot towel."

She grinned at me, and I grinned back. It was hard not to. I hadn't seen her in a long while, and since I'd last seen her, me and her both had grown quite a bit, and she'd grown in a real nice way.

I had been standing by the table, like a servant, but now I dipped me a cup of water from a bucket and sat down at the table with it.

"What you coming this way for?" I said.

"We come in the storm," Jane said.

"No you didn't," I said. "You couldn't have come in that storm."

"Did too," Tony said. "We darn near died doing it."

"You couldn't have," I said. "That storm was one of the worst I've seen."

"Ought to have seen it close up," he said.

"If it wasn't us that come in the storm," Jane said, "it was a couple looked just like us."

I shook my head. "I can't imagine how you did it."

"'Cause Sissy is smart," Tony said.

"Smart ain't got nothing to do with sand," I said, "and if she's so smart, what in the world has she got you two out in a sandstorm for in the first place?"

Tony turned and looked at Jane like this was a question he hadn't thought of and felt ought to be answered.

She said, "Well, it wasn't like we had a choice. The house was nearly blown flat. We could have stayed there in the ruins of it, I suppose, but I decided the better part of valor was to abandon it."

"The better part of valor?" I said.

"She reads books," Tony said, as if it was a thing he couldn't really explain.

"That's true," she said, "and someday I'm going to write for a real fine newspaper. The problem is I can't type. I'm going to find a school somewhere that can teach me, and then I'm going to be a journalist. But I'm going to look around first, learn a little about life."

"Journalist. That's what they call them that type on typewriters for newspapers," Tony said. He looked proud of himself for knowing that.

"Right now," Jane said, "I'm getting me and Tony out of this gritty hell. I'm going to take me and him somewhere else. We'll walk if we have to, but I thought it might be better if we drove Old Man Turpin's Ford."

"How in the world would you drive Old Man Turpin's Ford?" I asked "He ain't much of a loaner kind of person."

"Oh, well, we thought we'd borrow it," she said. "Sort of."

4

Now, before you figure Jane and Tony as just straightaway thieves, I think I ought to do a little explaining.

They told me how they came by their plan, and when I heard it, I sort of liked it and decided to count myself in. I had to. Neither of them could drive a car, and I could. We'd had one once, right up until a month before, when Daddy sold it to pay for some flour and such, and some medicine for Mama. I guess he knew right then that that was the end. When he took that car into town and gave it up for a few dollars, I seen the light go out of his eyes sure as if someone inside his head had pulled a light cord. He was near to being a dead man walking from then on. Only thing that kept him connected to life at all was Mama, and when she died, that was the end of it. If there were any lights left on anywhere inside him, they went dark right then, and that was all she wrote.

But the thing was, Old Man Turpin had a car, and he had died, which was something I didn't know. No one around our parts had known of him having any next of kin, so there wasn't anyone next in line for that automobile, and the way Jane explained it, it was a shame to let a good Ford stay under a tarp, get all rusted out and eventually full of dust.

Jane had a way of talking that could get you on her side of things, even when you were certain you weren't going to agree. I think it was all that reading she did. In her mouth, words were as sweet as candy or as sharp as razors, and she could switch from one to the other in midstream. She was one of them kind that loved to hear herself talk.

What I didn't know was Jane and Tony's mama had run off with a Bible salesman, and their daddy, not long after, had a tractor accident while trying to plow out some rows, long after there was any chance of things growing. Way Jane explained it, their dad was real stubborn, right up until the time his Poppin' Johnny tractor rocked over and caught him under it and squashed him like a bug.

They was going to try and bury him, but couldn't get him out from under the tractor. He was bedded down good in the sand with the tractor on top of him. Jane come up then with the idea just to shovel sand over him and the tractor, at least until they could have a proper burial, 'cause there were hungry dogs roving around. But the sandstorm had come up and they went into the house and Mother Nature covered him up for them.

Their house, which had mostly been supported by good luck and a prayer, finally blowed down, and they stayed in what was left of it for the night. Next morning they had to dig out a little, and once they were out, they figured their place was done for and they had to leave.

They decided to walk out and try to get some help so

maybe they could get their daddy buried proper and find a place to stay. Jane found a couple of her books that hadn't been blowed away or buried by the sand and put them in a pillowcase. As the storm hadn't hit yet when they did this, they headed out, got to Old Man Turpin's, and found him sitting in a rocking chair in his doorway, the door open. He was covered from head to foot in sand.

"It didn't take no wizard," Tony said, "to figure he was dead."

Jane nodded. "I figured he did it on purpose. Just didn't care anymore, sat out there and let the dust get him. We started looking around in the house. Everyone knows Old Man Turpin doesn't have any kin, so we knew we weren't going to disturb anyone. We got some flour sacks and put some things in them he wouldn't need anymore, like canned goods. I put my books in there with the cans, and we made us packs. Then we went out to his barn and found that Ford under a tarpaulin. Course, then we realized it didn't do us any good, 'cause neither of us could drive. We covered it up and started out this way, hoping to find somebody to help us, and then the storm hit."

"Why didn't you stay there? Turpin has a pretty good house."

"'Cause he was dead on the porch is one thing," Jane said, "and the other is staying there wasn't going to get us any farther than there."

"I thought you was just looking for some help to bury your pa?" I said.

"Was," she said. "At first. Then me and Tony got to thinking that Pa was pretty well covered up as it was, and

16

what we needed more than anything was just to be gone from here. I don't see no cause just to stay around and eat dirt and get old, if I even manage to get old. Way things are going, I'll be out on some porch somewhere in a chair with the dust covering me up. It's not much of a future, way I look at it."

"I suppose not," I said.

"So," Jane said. "We left out of there thinking we could find someone who could drive the car, but then we got caught up in another storm before we got very far. Just walking out there in all that dirt is some real trouble. There's still roads, but they're pretty covered up too. Not so much I don't think a car could make it. And if it can't, I'm still willing to give it a try, if I can get someone to drive."

"It wasn't for that old bridge over the creek, we'd have been done in just like Turpin," Tony said. "We crawled under there and pushed up against the bank. There wasn't no water in the creek, and we just listened to the wind blow all the morning, and watched that old dry bed get drier and fill up with sand. This afternoon when it was all winded out, we was still sitting, and that sand was over our ankles, but soon as it quit we started out walking, and it was like it was waiting on us to come out of hiding, because we hadn't gone more than a mile or two when the storm hit us again."

"Wasn't nothing for us to do but keep on coming," Jane said. "And we did. We knew if we lay down and waited somewhere, unless it was some good place like that bridge, we was done for, we'd never get up. We didn't have any real choice but to put our noses forward and our ears back, like plow mules, and just keep on coming."

"The wind blowed us down three or four times," Tony said.

"We found the old fence line that runs from the Thompson property to yours, and we clung to that where it was standing, and we crawled where it wasn't. When it was standing again, we took to it, and finally we come to your place and you come out to help us."

Jane paused and looked around.

"By the way," she said, "where's your folks?"

I took a deep breath and told them. I was pretty weak by the time I was done explaining.

The last thing I said was "I buried them together in the barn."

"You seem to be the only one of us that's any good at getting anyone buried," Tony said.

Jane just stared at me for a long time, long enough I could see how red-rimmed her eyes were and how the corners of her mouth was cracked from sand getting behind the scarf she'd had on.

"I'm real sorry, Jack," she said. "Looks like we're all orphans."

5

You never knew about the dust storms. Sometimes there wouldn't be any for a week; then there would be two in one day, or one that would last all day and through the night. Sometimes they went on for days at a time.

I thought over what Jane had said about Old Man Turpin's car, and though I ain't a thief, I began to think it was an idea that had some worth. Old Man Turpin wasn't exactly the friendliest soul who had ever lived. He might have had a wife and family once, but nobody knew of any, and nobody knew him to do anything but farm, and quite well, until the dust storms came and wiped everybody out.

A fella like that wasn't going to offer us his car, but I figured what we was talking about, being orphans and all and wanting to get out of Oklahoma, was just a form of borrowing. A wide form of it, but I made the whole thing agreeable in my head nonetheless. At least for the moment.

I had some bottles we could cork, and we went out to the barn and filled them, so as to try and have some water without dirt in it. Soon as we run the bottles full, we corked them and wrapped them in towels and put them in a flour sack. We used the pump then to get enough water to wipe our faces and hands and arms down. It was refreshing to be a little cleaner, if not exactly churchgoing in appearance.

But I will add this. With Jane washed up, and her having taken one of Mama's combs and combed her hair out, she looked good. Like a less clean version of some of those women I'd seen on the covers of magazines, but wearing pants and work boots. I felt a little funny looking at her, like maybe there was some kind of magic in her.

We got a few of the canned goods left in the kitchen and packed those too, and then we decided the thing to do was to wait until tomorrow. If the weather was good in the morning, and the sky in the distance didn't look like it had a line of storms coming, we'd head out as fast as we could go to Old Man Turpin's.

I slept in Mama and Daddy's bed and let Jane and Tony have my pallet in the corner. In the morning we got up and took a look outside. It looked okay.

There was a patch of scrub oaks that ran down by the dry bed of a long-gone creek behind the house. It went a long ways in the direction of Turpin's place, and that seemed to me to be the way to go. The trees and the creek bank would give us some protection against any sudden storm that might come up, and it was shaded a little. It wasn't perfect, but it was a plan of some sort.

We went down behind the house with our bags, and it was hard going until we got near the creek bed. The trees had kept some of the sand out, though they were ragged trees. The grasshoppers and birds had stripped all the leaves, and deer and lost cattle had chewed a lot of the bark. It was a bony kind of shade, but it was shade.

The creek was still dry, but we could walk there better than anywhere else because the bottom of it had been full of rocks, and even with the sand on top, it was fairly solid. The sky was as blue as a Jimmy Rogers song. There wasn't a cloud in the heavens. The wind wasn't blowing and the sun was high and hot and we were sweaty and tired by the time it was late afternoon and we come up behind Old Man Turpin's house.

When we got there, we went around to the front porch, and just like Jane and Tony said, the porch was covered in sand, except where they had made a path to the front door. Old Man Turpin was in his chair, though you couldn't tell it was him or a chair unless you looked real hard. He was just a big mound of sand mostly the color of Oklahoma, with a bit of Nebraska and a lot of Texas worked in, and I'm pretty sure Kansas was swirled in there too.

On the porch I brushed some dirt away from his face, and the first thing I seen was a corncob pipe in his mouth, the bowl all filled with sand. I scraped some more, and then I could see the brim of his hat mashed into his face. He had his eyes closed and his mouth open, and there was sand all in it, like someone had stood there and poured it into him with a funnel. He had drowned in dirt.

"See," Tony said. "He's deader'n an anvil."

"He is, at that," I said.

I guess we was being pretty casual about death, but for the last couple of years it had been all around us, and as of recent, up close and personal. It was the sort of thing that stunned you at the same time it made you feel as empty as a corn crib after the rats had been in it.

When we got inside the house, I was glad we had brought water, because there was none there. While Jane and Tony laid out some things from our bag so we could eat, I went out to the well and saw that it had filled in with sand. I figured that was why Old Man Turpin had given up. No water. No hope.

Back in the house, we sat down at the table and ate some peaches from cans. We drank some of the water we had brought, then we went outside to the barn to look at the Ford.

Like they'd said, it was under a tarp, so we pulled it off. Sometimes dust storms blew so hard they built up static electricity. Back when we had a car, I seen Daddy go out after a sandstorm, and even though the car was in the barn, enough dust had blown in and over it that when he touched the car door, it knocked him down like a lighting strike. He was dazed for half the day, and considered himself lucky not to have been killed.

So I was careful when I touched the Ford, kind of popping my hand in first, like a snake striking a mouse. When I hit the handle, nothing. I opened the door and looked around for the key, found it stuck up by the sun visor. I tried it and the car started right up without no trouble. Luckily, the gauge showed there was plenty of gas, so we was ready to go. Provided I didn't wrap the car around a tree.

"Hot dog," Tony said. "We can get out of this place."

I turned off the car.

I said, "Don't you think we ought to bury Old Man Turpin?"

Jane put out a hand and leaned on the car. It was black, and though it had been covered tight with the tarp, there was still a faint film of dust all over it. When she moved her hand, her print stayed there. She said, "With us taking his car and burying him too, it might look worse than if we just leave him."

"We could drop him in that old dry well," Tony said. "It would look like he fell in."

"We won't do no such thing," I said. "I ain't no criminal. I'm just taking this car 'cause there ain't any other choices. Sometime soon enough we can tell someone we took it. Maybe."

"No one is going to miss it unless they come out to see him," Jane said. "And I guess they will. Somebody has to miss him for something sometime. But he never liked anyone and no one really liked him. We wouldn't have come here if we didn't have to."

"It was kind of nice he was dead," Tony said. "It made it easier to take his stuff."

"Shush, now," Jane said. "It wasn't like that at all."

"Well," Tony said, "it was kind of like that."

"We could leave a note," I said, "explaining things. We could say where we buried him and that we took the car, and that we did it because we felt we didn't have a choice."

"That's no good," Jane said.

"I think it is," I said, and I went back into the house and

23

left a note that said what we was doing, and how we didn't bury him 'cause we thought people ought to know right where he was, case he was going to a graveyard instead of a plot next to his house. I wrote as best I could how my parents was buried in the barn, and how the property was pretty near being the bank's anyway, and how they could have it.

I didn't like the idea of the bank owning my kin's bodies, but I had always been taught it wasn't the body that mattered, it was the life inside it. That life was long gone now.

While I was finishing the note, Jane come up, Tony lagging along behind her.

"We really shouldn't wait around," Jane said. "We should start trying to make some real ground before another storm settles in. We're fed and we got a car and we're ready to go, and I say we should go."

"Dang right," Tony said.

I wasn't all that certain it was the right thing to do, but I was pretty certain it was the only thing to do.

Back at the car, we put our bags of goods on the back floorboard. Jane got in on the front passenger side, and Tony rode in the backseat. There was plenty of room for him and the goods, and even some room left over for another two boys just Tony's size. That was some big Ford.

I backed us out of the barn and bumped along over the sand. It was slow going, but it was going.

And I won't lie—theft or not, it felt pretty good to know I had a V8 Ford and my foot on the gas, and that I was driving away from all that death and all that sand, pushing on forward with some kind of hope. I didn't know right then where I was going. But I knew one thing for sure.

Wherever I was going in that stolen Ford, I was darn sure going to try to get there fast.

6

It was a long time before we found any kind of ruts we could ride in, but when we did, we started moving faster, and I got a little braver about my driving. Course, I had to hope I didn't grind the gears so much I burned up the clutch or tore up the engine in some way, or ran off into a ditch and killed us all.

Jane kept saying stuff like "I thought you said you could drive."

"I said I could drive, but I didn't say I was any good at it. I ain't Henry Ford his ownself. I'm just me."

"I see that," Jane said.

"I think he does all right," Tony said. In that moment, I liked him a lot.

"It's all right if you look where you're going," she said. "Nobody is going to give you points for guesswork."

We rode along like that for a while, and I started taking in the sights, such as they were. It was mostly dust, and every field looked just like the others. There were some fences standing, but most of them were pushed down by the sand and the wind, and a few were leaning and about to go. There were a number of dead rattlesnakes hanging off the barbwire fences. There were a lot of folks around them parts had Cherokee blood in them, my family being one of them. Cherokee believed if you killed a rattlesnake and put it so it could be seen, the gods would give rain. So far, them that believed that had been wrong, and the only thing that had come of it was a lot of dead snakes.

After we had driven for a while, I said, "Maybe if we're going to run off somewhere, we ought to know where it is we're going."

"Away from here," Tony said. "That's good enough."

"I'm for deciding which way to go," I said as the car bumped along. "Any kind of idea might be good, since so far, nobody has one."

"I don't know about that," Jane said. "Seems to me I'm the only decisive one in the bunch. Wasn't for me, you'd still be at home alone, and Tony here would have stayed under a collapsed house till what food there was run out and he dried up and blew away."

"That's probably true," Tony said.

Actually, she had a point, but she still didn't have a direction. I decided to take the bull by the horns.

"California?" I said. "How about we go there? They got work, and we're all able-bodied enough to work."

"I'm kind of a runt," Tony said.

"They don't make no difference in age or size in the fields," I said. "You can stand on a stool to pick an orange, or get down on your knees to dig a tater."

"I was hoping for a brain-using job," Tony said.

"I wouldn't hold my breath on that one," I said.

"Not long ago, Pa was in town talking to a fella who had come back from California," Jane said. "Took his whole family. Was gone two months. He said it wasn't the paradise you'd think. They called everybody that come out there Okies, even if they wasn't from here. People got beat and robbed and taken advantage of, and with so many folks scrambling for jobs, there weren't many to be had. He come back to Oklahoma, though he said it was like it was when he left. He wanted to go somewhere else, but his truck broke down and they couldn't go nowhere else unless they walked. He said the oranges in California was fresh, though, and it was real green."

"We need more than oranges, and greenery is nice to look at, but the main green we need is dollar green," I said.

"In my bag," Jane said, "I got fifteen dollars saved. It'll be a start."

"I got a dollar," Tony said. "What you got, Jack?"

"Pocket lint."

"So," Jane said, "we got sixteen dollars and some pocket lint."

"But we got high hopes," I said. "We're all ready to conquer the world, except we don't know where we're going."

"I always heard we had kin in East Texas, around Tyler," Jane said, looking out the side window. "I don't know them none, but I think they're an aunt and an uncle. If we could find them, they might give us some kind of help."

"I ain't never heard of them," Tony said.

"That's because it never came up when you were around."

"All right, then," I said. "Which way do you figure is East Texas from here?"

"I'd go south first, and then when we get to Texas, veer east."

"Point taken," I said.

7

We eventually found a pretty good road. Driving along, we passed a couple of old trucks packed down with all manner of goods, heading out of Oklahoma. As we did, I seen the drivers was men wearing old hats and a touch of beard. They was missing teeth and had expressions so sad it made my heart hurt just looking at them. They looked like those husks of insects you find after spiders have sucked the juice out of them. In those faces was dead children and blowed-away farms and buried dreams, and like us, I figured they didn't have no true direction. Just an urge to get away and hope there was something beyond their view from the windshield.

We come upon a little town. I hadn't never been there before. I had been to Hootie Hoot, which was the closest town to us, but this one, which was called Ferguson, was new to me. Thing was, I hadn't never been any farther in this direction than the back of our forty acres. The Catchers weren't by nature much on traveling, especially since traveling costs money. But here I was, a regular family renegade, on the road and rolling forward.

While we was riding into town, Jane said, "I think we ought to stop here and use some money to eat at a café. That will be our treat. Then we can buy a few goods at the store to take with us, and from then on we can eat on the way, stopping beside the road to picnic."

"We brought goods," I said.

"Those are our emergency goods," she said. "And we should get some gas."

"We got plenty of gas," I said.

"An emergency thinker stays ready and prepared. If we fill it now, we won't have to worry for a long while. We don't know what's up the road, Jack. Let's top it off."

For some reason, I was starting to do whatever she wanted. It annoyed me, but I couldn't keep from doing it.

I saw a gas station, so I pulled over by the pump and got out and looked around until I found the tank on the car. I had never put gas in a car. Daddy had always done the job, so I didn't even know for sure where it went in.

An old man with no teeth came out and grinned some gums at me. He said, "How much gas you wanting?"

I hadn't considered, but Jane was out and coming around the back end of the car. She said, "Give us two dollars, if it'll hold it, and can you check the oil and water and get the windshield? Might check the air in the tires too."

"Yes, ma'am, I can do that," he said, glancing into the car at Tony. "You kids running away from home or something? Are you a family and that's your little boy?"

"Really," Jane said. "Do we look old enough to be parents of a boy that size?"

"No, but it's a conversation starter," the old man said.

"We ain't got no parents," I said. "We're off to East Texas. We think."

"You think?"

"We're a little fuzzy on directions," I said. "I know you got to go south before you go east, but that's about it. And I know that because she told me."

"You ain't running from the law, are you?" the old man said.

"Heavens no," Jane said. "We're brothers and sister. And this car is the family car. Our kin is all dead. The dirty pneumonia got them all. You want to know something else that stinks? Dang dog died the same day the cows stopped giving milk and the chickens quit laying. Ain't that something? Only thing missing was dropping our last dollar down a rat hole."

I had suspicions all along, but now they were confirmed.

Jane was a born liar. And though she was a natural at it, good as anyone I'd ever heard, she was also one that didn't like to quit if she had a good audience. She kept right on painting the barn, so to speak, when there wasn't no need for paint, or for that matter when the paint bucket was empty. She wasn't just a liar and a thief, she had turned me into both, and it was my fault because I'd let her.

"We've got a few dollars and some goods, but not much," she said, "and we're going to East Texas to find relatives, if they'll have us. We're all talented singers, and think we might form a family group with us and the relatives, like the Carter Family. Only we got a real high tenor in the boy there, and that will make us unique."

She nodded at Tony. He smiled and waved.

"Well now," said the old man, eyeing Tony through the window, as if he might want to burn the image of him on to his brain so he could tell folks he had seen a high tenor up close, "that's quite the business. You know, this car looks familiar to me. Do you know a fellow named Otto Turpin?"

Jane pursed her lips and looked up a bit, like she was giving it some serious thought, shook her head slowly, said, "Nope. Can't say I do. You, Eugene?"

It took me a second to realize that she had christened me with that name.

"No," I said. "It don't ring a bell."

The old man nodded. "Yeah, well, tell you what, wait right here while I get my tire gauge, and then I'll get your gas."

When the old man was back inside the station, I said,

31

"What'd you have to tell him all that for? And call me Eugene?"

Jane wasn't listening to me. "He recognized the car. He knows we're thieves."

She went quickly to the door of the station, looked in, and came back.

"He went out the back door," she said. "I bet he's going to get some kind of law, though what it would be in this little hole is beyond me."

She went around and got in on her side of the car, and by then I figured out that we was leaving, and in a hurry.

I cranked up the Ford and we got back on the road, and as soon as we was to the city limits sign, which took about two minutes, I jammed my foot down on the gas. The road was a main road, and the county had worked at scraping it clear of dust mounds, and for the first time I began to open up and feel the throb of the engine through the steering wheel, the power of that big machine.

8

"They're going to go check on Turpin," I said, "and when they find him dead, they're going to think we murdered him."

"Murdered him?" Jane said. "And how did we do that? Piled sand on top of him while he sat there rocking, smoking his pipe? No. Even the locals around here won't be that dumb."

"You're one of the locals," I said.

"Yeah," she said, "but I can read."

"So can I."

"What? *Tractor Digest?*"

"You ain't been to school any more than me. And there ain't no school no more. We ain't had school in more than a year. Ain't no school to go to. Storms shut it down."

"The teacher teaches in her own home," Tony said. "I went there to stay away from Pa. He had a hankering to whip my butt now and then for entertainment. So school's better."

"That's right," Jane said. "And I went to school because I value an education."

"It's certainly doing you a lot of good right now," I said.

"You've left two men dead, stolen a car, and now we're running from the law."

Jane turned and looked through the back windshield.

"By the time that old man tells the law, we're out of his town. And by the time he can get word to the county, we'll be long gone."

She turned front again. "It's like in them movies where the cowboy crosses the Rio Grande and is free."

"We're going to Mexico?" I said.

"No," she said, "course not. We're going to East Texas. I was speaking in a metaphorical way."

"You were?" I said.

"You wouldn't understand. Teacher taught that after you stopped coming."

9

We drove all day.

I thought about Old Man Turpin as we drove. I wondered how he afforded such a nice car. It wasn't but a couple years old and didn't look to have been driven all that much. I wondered what he thought about when he was alone in his house with his new Ford in the barn and no place to go and his supper on the table with no one to share it with.

He wasn't a friendly man—he wouldn't even wave at you if he passed you on the street in town. If he did speak to you, it was usually to complain. He once stopped me on the street to tell me I ought not to eat a peppermint stick while I was walking 'cause I might fall down and it might punch through the top of my mouth and stick me in the brain.

I thought that a little unlikely. I also thought he probably didn't care if I was brain-stabbed or not. It was just something to complain about. Like Mama used to say about mean folks, they've always got some kind of pain of their own, and they don't mind sharing it.

It must have been that way for him to finally give up and sit on his porch in his rocking chair and let blowing sand that cut like buckshot cover him up while he tried to smoke his pipe. Something like that wasn't any kind of accident. You had to be dedicated to it.

But all that said, he traveled some. At least as far as that filling station behind us. The old man had recognized the car. Heck, for all I knew, Turpin was a big man around town there. I don't guess you really know nothing about nobody unless you walk around in their shoes some.

I found a station in a town some fifty miles out of Ferguson, and we got gas there, but we didn't stop at a café to eat because we was on the run and couldn't afford time or money for such foolishness now. Jane bought us some pickled eggs from a big jar in the station and some Cokes, and we ate and drank while I drove.

No one had recognized the car at the station, as far as we could tell, so I figured that Ferguson was about as far south as Old Man Turpin went. Or at least, I hoped so. He didn't strike me as a world traveler, any more than we was.

As we rode, I looked alongside the roads and saw the sand piled there, and beyond the edge of the roads was more sand. It reminded me of pictures I had seen in schoolbooks of the Arabian Desert, and it occurred to me that I had near forgot how things had looked before the great winds had come and picked up all the good earth and thrown it to the sky. Thrown it up there and whirled it around, sorted out what good topsoil remained—and that wasn't much—and then chucked it all over Oklahoma and beyond. It was hard to remember how things had looked when the woods were thick and the fields were high with green corn and rows of shiny green beans and peanuts and potato tops thick and standing up tall, letting you know if you dug down under them, you'd find some fat potatoes for cleaning, cutting, and frying. Peanuts to parch and crack and eat raw. Plenty of peas to pick and boil up with a chunk of pork rind. All gone now.

It was hard to remember the last time I was truly clean. When there wasn't any dust under my collar, behind or in my ears, or in my hair. It was hard to remember being able to walk to school, or darn near anywhere except a field, and not have to stop to pour dust out of your shoes.

It was hard to remember when all the earth hadn't been thrown to the sky.

I thought on all these things as I drove, and I have to admit, it was both bitter and sweet, but it was nice to have my head free of Jane's words for a while. After the pickled egg and the Coca-Cola, she had grown silent—a condition that I figured was unnatural to her, and on some level didn't suit her, but right then I was grateful for it.

The sand didn't come during the day, and by the time we took an old road off the main highway and parked alongside a creek that actually had water in it, under an oak that actually had leaves, it was near nightfall.

The trail wound down off the road and under the tree in such a way we were well out of eyeshot from the highway, but not so deep down we couldn't be back up there in fifteen minutes.

We had a number of goods we'd brought, and one of those was a small pot. We put that aside, gathered sticks, and made a stack of little ones for tinder and bigger ones for real fuel, and we did all this under the oak tree. We put matches to the sticks and started a fire. Next we opened a can of beans and heated them up in the pot. We dipped the beans out of the pot with a cup, put them in the wooden bowls we had. We each had our own spoon, and had even been smart enough to bring some pepper and salt. The beans wasn't like Mama used to make them, as they was canned beans we'd had to fight open with a can opener, but they tasted pretty good just the same.

We drank from our bottles of water and then set around in silence with our backs against the tree.

I don't know how long we sat there, but I do know it was

good and dark when we went up to the car. Tony stretched out on the backseat, and I sat behind the wheel and slid the seat back and tried to sleep. Jane leaned against the door on her side.

The moon was bright that night, and it was shining in on her, and the way the light was on her face, she looked like pictures I'd seen of Joan of Arc, or maybe it was someone else, but whoever it was, she was pretty.

I watched her sleep for a while, and then I nodded and went to sleep myself.

In the morning, when I woke up, things didn't seem as bad as they had the night before.

I got out of the car as silently as I could, walked down to the creek.

It was a wide creek, and unlike those near my home, it was full of water, and the water was running fast. I walked along the creek till I came to a place where it went narrow and was partly fed by a spring. The spring bubbled up out of the ground and ran into the creek and joined up with water coming from some other source. My guess was it was the Red River, as we were heading in the direction of the Texas border. Or so I hoped. So far we were mostly working off the sun's position and a lot of guesswork and wishful thinking.

I walked back along the bank and enjoyed the cool morning air and the greenery and the way the boughs grew close and shaded things. The trees that grew against the bank had thick roots, and they twisted out from the soil like well ropes and hung over the water. Watching the creek as I walked, I saw fish in the water. They were small, but they were fish.

I found a little willow growing up along the bank, and I got hold of it, bent it back and forth till it snapped off, and then used my pocketknife to clean it of smaller limbs. I cleaned it until I had a fishing pole.

Back at the car, I tried to open the back door as gently as I could. When I did, Tony stirred, looked at me, then turned his face into the seat and went back to sleep. Jane didn't stir.

I lifted our flour sacks out, two in one hand, one in the other, and carried them down to the oak by the creek. I dug around in one of the bags until I found a ball of twine, and measured me off some and cut it and tied it to the bottom of the pole, ran it to the tip, and let the bulk of it hang. I bent a safety pin I had in place of a button on my shirt, made a hook, and tied it to the twine. I got the empty bean can from last night's supper and walked along the creek until I saw some soft dirt up on a rise. It was good dirt, not sand. It was the kind of dirt that needed to be in the fields. It was the kind of dirt they had farmed out and scraped off the top of the earth, leaving only the bad earth, the sand that the wind could carry off as easy as if it were talcum powder.

I dug in the dirt with my hands, and it felt good to put my fingers in it. It was rich and full, and it would grow corn as high as a rain cloud. I didn't know till right then how much I wanted to be away from dried-out Oklahoma. It was like I had been numb until this moment when my fingers went into the dirt. I was feeling things again. Smelling things again, like the rich dark earth and the sharp smell of the trees in the grove. In that moment, the sky seemed bluer and the sun seemed brighter, and at least for a little bit, it seemed as if there might be a brighter tomorrow. My mama always said that. No matter how bad things were, there was always tomorrow, and a possibility it would be brighter. Daddy hadn't remembered that, but I told myself right then and there that I would.

Eventually, I found some worms. Some of them were grubs. I liked grubs the best for fishing, so I was glad to have them. I filled the can and went back to my fishing line lying beneath the oak. I cut another stretch of twine off the ball and wadded it up and stuffed it in my pocket. I put one of the grubs on the hook I had made from the safety pin and went along the bank with my can and pole until I came to where it was wide enough I couldn't jump across and deep enough I could have stood in it to my waist. I put my line in there, and found shade beneath a sweet gum that was full with leaves and sat with my back against it.

Daddy and I had gone fishing a bunch of times, and I thought about him while I fished, and without even knowing it was coming, I started to cry. I thought about Mama, and how she would fry the fish after we cleaned them. How after a meal like that, Daddy would churn up some ice cream and we'd sit out on the porch with it in big bowls and eat it and watch lightning bugs fly along.

Mama would put her arm around me, and tell me stories, mostly things her parents had told her. Scotch-Irish stories from the old country about ghosts and leprechauns and such. She told me her parents had died of the smallpox, both of them, when she was a girl. She said a day never passed she didn't think about them.

Mama always smelled like she had just taken a bath, and her breath was sweet as mint. She never missed telling me she loved me. I tried to remember if I had told her I loved her before she died. I wanted to believe I had.

When I was young, when it rained, I didn't like the lightning and the thunder, and she would lie down beside me and tell me it wasn't nothing more than a bunch of little men throwing balls at bowling pins, and that was the noise I heard, and the fire I seen in the sky was just them lighting their pipes.

It seemed so long ago.

I couldn't remember the last time I'd seen a lightning bug.

Or rain.

And I didn't remember what ice cream tasted like.

All of a sudden, I was crying. It came on hard, with me heaving and bawling like a lost calf. I was glad there wasn't anyone around to hear me, and when I was through crying, I dipped some water in my palm from the creek and washed my face with it. After that, I was mostly all right.

I don't know how long I fished, because I dozed a little, but eventually I felt a tug. I pulled up a little perch. I took it off the hook and laid it out on the soft ground, where it flopped around. It was what we called a sun perch, bright with colors and small in length, but pretty fat. I baited the hook again.

Sticking the pole in the dirt so that the line hung in the water, I took the twine out of my pocket and got the perch and ran the cord through its gills, then took it down to the creek and lowered it in on the twine. I tied the twine off to a root sticking out of the bank and went back to fishing.

By the time the sun was up high, I had four perch. I wanted to catch one more, but by then they had quit biting, and I wasn't up for walking along the creek and trying to find another spot.

I took the fish and gutted them and cleaned them in the cold spring water. I built a fire and got a frying pan out of the flour sack, along with a can of lard. I scooped some lard into the frying pan with my spoon, and when the lard was melting I put the fish in the pan. There wasn't any flour and egg to make a batter, but they'd fry up good just the same.

One of Jane's books was in one of the bags, and I got it out to read. It was a book of poems. I wasn't much on poems, but I read it anyway. I found it was good to move the words around in my mouth and my mind. It had been a while since I had done that, and I had pretty well forgot the fun of reading. I read and smelled the fish fry, pausing now and then to turn them in the lard with my spoon, since we hadn't been smart enough to bring forks. The smell was starting to make me hungry, and my stomach was growling like a tiger.

I got some salt and pepper and dosed the fish a little with it, and by the time Jane and Tony were awake and come drifting down the hill to the smell of the perch, they were fried up and ready.

When Jane saw that I had been reading her book, she said, "That isn't *Tractor Digest*."

I didn't say anything to that. I just put the book back in the sack.

"That smells good," Tony said.

"It's for all of us," I said. "Get your plates and spoons."

We had the fish for breakfast, and they were good, if I say so myself.

And I do.

10

Just about the time I was thinking things weren't turning out so bad after all, events took a turn for the worse.

I was driving along, and we'd actually been singing songs together, some Carter Family stuff, and though we weren't too good as singers on the whole, Jane wasn't bad by herself at all. I liked hearing her sing. She had a high sweet voice that cut the air like a sharp knife and then came floating down soft as a kitten's belly.

She had taken off on a solo, and I was enjoying it, when we blew a tire. The car sort of bunny-hopped, then skidded, and I fought that wheel all over the place. Next thing I knew we had the back tire off in a ditch and the car was rocking like it was going to lean over on its side and die a hard death with us inside it.

I turned off the engine and got out, and Jane slid out on my side. Tony climbed out too, and we stood looking at the car like we were watching a great ship sink. The back right tire was blown out, and there was rubber all over the road.

"That one's gone," Tony said, like nobody could have figured that out without his help.

I touched the car, and it rocked. If I tried to get the spare tire and tools out of the turtle hull and change the flat, I figured the whole car would just turn over in the ditch. It was a big ditch. Wide and deep.

"Well, what now?" Jane said, as if everything we had done was my idea, and I personally had thrown tacks in the road to blow out the tire.

"I ain't got no idea," I said.

We stood there for about fifteen minutes, trying to will the car back on the road so we could fix the tire, but that wasn't getting anything done. I was thinking on an idea that might work, if I held my mouth just right and the ground didn't shift. Most likely, it was an idea that would end up with me in the ditch, under the car, with the blown-out tire and wheel lying down on my chest.

In other words, it wasn't an idea that charmed me much, but I was considering on it. I thought I could drag enough limbs out of a pecan grove across the way, stack them in the ditch tight enough so that the blown tire could rest on it, and then drive the car out. It had about as much chance of working as me bending a tree over and getting on it, letting it go, and shooting myself to the moon.

I was about to suggest we start dragging limbs, when we looked up to the sound of an engine. A brown Buick was coming our way. Smoke was curling up from under the hood and filling the air, and I could smell something burning from where we were.

"Looks like we ain't the only ones with car trouble," Tony said.

I could see two men. One behind the wheel, the other sitting over on the passenger side. Even through the windshield, I thought they looked like hard men, and the closer they got, the more I was certain of it.

They stopped the car at the edge of the road next to the ditch. Nobody got out for a while. The car sat there and steamed white smoke from under its hood. Finally a man in a brown suit with blue pinstripes got out of the car. He had a light beige shirt on and a big wide tie that was mostly brown with blue designs on it. The way he stretched his leg to get out of the car, I saw he was wearing some two-tone shoes, brown and white, and brown socks with blue clocks on them.

He came forward about halfway between his car and ours, stopped and stared at us, and grinned. He was a nice-looking fella with a square-jawed face. He wasn't wearing a hat. His dark brown hair was freshly cut. He had a toothpick in his mouth, and he was moving it back and forth over his teeth with his tongue like it was a dog looking for a place to lie down. He had an expression on his face like he'd heard a joke he liked but he wasn't going to share it.

The other man got out on the passenger side. He was in his shirtsleeves. The shirt was lilac-colored and the rest of what he wore was black. He didn't have on a tie. He looked a lot more pleasant than the driver.

Both men came over to us. The one in shirtsleeves said, "You kids seem to be in a fix."

"From what I can tell," Jane said, "and understand, I'm not a mechanic, but I'd say you got a busted radiator, and from the way your car sounds you might be just shy of a rocker arm going out."

The man in the pinstripe suit laughed. He said, "No one can miss that the radiator has blown out, but you don't know from rocker arms."

"I guess I don't know much, but I don't like you coming up here smirking like you're about to lay out some real mechanic advice or something, and you can't even fix your own car."

"Well now," said the man in pinstripes. "I was actually thinking along those lines myself. I don't plan on fixing nothing. I was just thinking how damn lucky we are to come up on you, you with a car that don't need nothing but a tire, and us with a car that is going to have to be either replaced or jacked up and another car driven under it."

"How would that work?" Tony said.

The man moved the toothpick to the other side of his mouth. "That's what we call an expression, kid."

"I know what you mean," Jane said. "Tony ain't nothing but a kid. But I know what you mean. I think even Jack might know."

I thought: Nice.

"Well then," said the man in the pinstripe suit, "since you know I can't jack our car up and drive another one under it, then you got to know that what I'm planning on is taking your car away from you. How about that, Little Snooty? Did you know that?"

"This isn't your car to take," Jane said, going closer to the man.

I said, "Jane. Don't."

"Yeah," said Pinstripe, reaching out and clutching Jane's face with his hand. "Don't, Jane."

She kicked him right between the legs. It was a good kick too. I figured if she'd kicked a potato she would have knocked it over their car and down the road a bit. It was such a hard kick, it sort of made me feel bad. It made him spit his toothpick out like he was shooting a bullet.

Even Tony went, "Holy moly."

Pinstripe let out a bellow and his eyes nearly closed, like he was squinting them against a harsh light he hoped would pass. He dropped to his knees.

The man in shirtsleeves let out a laugh, like he'd just seen a circus monkey do something funny.

"Damn, if that wasn't a good one," he said.

"I'll say," Tony said. "I've seen her do it before."

I took hold of Tony's arm and tried to shush him, but Jane wasn't finished.

"You ain't seen nothing yet," Jane said.

Pinstripe, still on his knees, pulled back his jacket and showed us a gun in a holster. He reached across and put his hand on it.

I was going to yell "Run," when the other man said to Pinstripe, "Put it up, you idiot. They're just a bunch of ragged kids."

11

"You got some spunk, kid," the man in shirtsleeves said, and gave Jane a smile.

"What I got is a size-four shoe with a good solid toe on it," Jane said. "And I suppose I put about two of the four in him."

Pinstripe finally got to his feet. He was mad enough to chew nails and spit horseshoes. The other man said, "Ah, come on, Timmy, where's your sense of humor?"

"Watch how much I laugh when I shoot her a couple times," Timmy said.

"Come on now," the other man said. "We ain't got time for this kind of silly business."

"It don't take so much time to shoot somebody," Timmy said. "And besides, I'd enjoy it."

"What you're going to do is shut up and help me get this car out of the ditch," said the man.

Timmy looked at him like he might not like that idea, but the way the other man was looking at him, and him not even having a gun, showed us who was boss pretty quick.

"Oh, it's all right," Timmy said. "I wasn't going to do nothing. I was just sore, is all."

"Consider yourself healed," said the man. "Go see how Buddy's doing."

Timmy went back to the car, opened a back door, and stood there talking. We couldn't hear what he was saying, but now we knew someone was in the backseat, lying down.

"Thanks," I said to the man. "Thanks for not letting him hurt us."

"Don't get too happy about things," he said. "I might let him shoot you yet. I ain't for killing for nothing, but my killing for something might be less than someone else's. He had that kick coming. But him I know, and you I don't have any idea about, and don't want one. Only concern I got for you is we might need you for something."

Timmy came back then. "Buddy ain't doing so good, Tiger."

"All right," the one called Tiger said. "We got to make some tough choices."

Tiger looked at us.

Jane said, "You wouldn't be Bad Tiger Malone, would you?"

"I would."

"Dang it," she said.

"What I want you kids to do is go back there and help Buddy out of the backseat. There's a little sycamore tree over there in the pasture, and I'd like you to help him over there so he can sit under it. You understand me?"

"Sure," I said. "We understand."

"What's wrong with him?" Jane asked.

49

"He's got a stomachache," Timmy said.

Bad Tiger looked down the road, first one way, then the other.

"We ain't got all day," Bad Tiger said. "I'll just keep the squirt here till you get back, 'cause I want you to come back, and right away." He reached out and took hold of Tony, resting his hand firmly on his shoulder. "I wouldn't want you to take too long or run off, 'cause I'd consider that bad behavior, and Tony here, he'd have to pay for your bad behavior. You wouldn't like that, would you, Tony?"

"Pay how?" Tony asked.

"Let's just say it would be harsh," Bad Tiger said.

"Yeah," Tony said. "Y'all come right back."

Timmy smiled. "Or take your time. Run off, you want to. I'll take care of Tony. I wouldn't mind that at all. When I get through with him, y'all can use what's left of him for third base or something."

"We'll hurry fast as we can," I said.

"Naw, don't hurry," Bad Tiger said. "Buddy's going to need your help. But don't hang on the clock hands, if you know what I mean."

"We know," Jane said. She was sounding a little subdued for the first time.

We went over to the Buick. The back door was still open. We looked in and saw a man stretched across the seat. His feet were on our side. His head was on the armrest across the way. His hair was down on his forehead, and it was wet with sweat. His face was beaded up with it, and his bloody gray suit jacket and tie lay on the floorboard. He had his hand on his stomach and he was breathing heavy. The seat and floor-board of the car were covered in blood.

A coat to match the pants Bad Tiger was wearing was slung across the front seat. A gun in a harness was there too.

The man in the seat saw me look at it. "I wouldn't, kid. It won't do you no good. Timmy would shoot you before you could get it pointed. And you'd have to be good just to get that far."

I didn't say anything. I just looked away from the gun.

"What's wrong with you?" Jane asked.

"Didn't you hear?" said Buddy. "I got a stomachache."

"We heard," she said, "but that's some stomachache. There's blood running between your fingers."

"That don't make it any less of a stomachache," he said.

"We're supposed to help you out and put you under a sycamore tree," I said.

Buddy sighed. "Yeah, I heard. I guess you better help me."

It took some work, and he screamed a couple times, but we got him to a sitting position. Jane got on one side and I got on the other. We put his arms over our shoulders and tried to walk him into the pasture toward the sycamore tree.

Sometimes he walked all right, and sometimes he stumbled.

"You better let me stop for a moment," he said. "Let me get my breath."

We stopped.

I heard Bad Tiger yell out, "Might as well just move on, Buddy. It ain't going to get no better."

"I reckon not," Buddy said, and we started moving again.

We got him to the sycamore and helped him sit down under it. He breathed a little more heavily.

"You feel any better?" I asked.

"Course not, kid. I got a bullet in me."

Jane spoke so only the three of us could hear. "Bad Tiger Malone is a bank robber. He's almost as famous as Pretty Boy Floyd."

"That's him, all right," Buddy said. "We hit a bank. Things didn't go well. I got shot and someone else got the money."

"Someone else?" I said.

"Forget it," he said. "I ain't up for conversation. Just keep me company awhile."

"He told us not to," Jane said. "He said he'd hurt my little brother."

"He can be all right sometimes," Buddy said. "Until he isn't all right. You'd think Timmy is the crazy one, but he's just less calm. Tiger, he's the one you got to watch."

"You seem nice enough," Jane said. "What are you doing with them?"

"I'm not nice, and I'm with them because I was raised bad. I've known Tiger since we was kids. He wasn't raised bad. He's just bad. Timmy, I don't know nothing other than I don't like him. I really should have taken up some other line of work."

"We're sorry you're hurt," I said.

"Yeah," Buddy said. "Me too."

"You coming back up here," Bad Tiger called, "or do I twist this kid's arm off and beat him with it?"

52

"We're coming," I called back.

"I'm sorry," Jane said. "We got to go."

"Ah, that's all right," Buddy said. "It can't be helped."

"What about you?" Jane asked.

"It is what it is," he said.

"But who'll take care of you?" Jane asked.

Buddy snorted, and then laughed. "Oh, I'll be taken care of, all right. You can count on that, missy."

12

We went back to the car, and Bad Tiger let go of Tony.

"How's Buddy doing?" Bad Tiger asked.

"Not so good," I said.

"Yeah, well," Bad Tiger said, "that's how I figured it."

"A stomach shot," Timmy said, "that don't do nobody any good. Not even a little bit."

"That seems like an understatement," Jane said.

"Girlie," Timmy said, "you better shut your mouth before I shut it for you."

Jane went silent, but I could tell it was paining her to do it.

"Would you say Buddy is going to get better?" Bad Tiger said to her.

"Not without some medical help," Jane said. "You could leave him with us. Maybe we can stop someone that comes along the road."

"Naw," Bad Tiger said. "Can't do that. I need you three for a while, and I don't want you talking to nobody on the road. And I figure you're right. Without a doctor he ain't getting no better."

Bad Tiger looked at Timmy.

"I got it," Timmy said.

Timmy went out across the pasture. We watched him walk to the sycamore tree. He said something to Buddy we couldn't understand. But we could hear Buddy.

"I hate to die in a bloody shirt," he said.

"That's just the way it is," Timmy said. We could hear him clearly this time.

"I reckon so. Well, get it over with," Buddy said.

We stood there stunned. I kind of knew what was coming but couldn't believe it was about to happen.

Bad Tiger said, "Why don't you kids turn and look down the road there."

We did just that.

And then we heard the shot.

"All right, then," Bad Tiger said, and we turned around.

Timmy came walking back toward us. I could see Buddy lying out by the sycamore tree.

Jane looked right at Bad Tiger and said, "You ain't nothing but the lowest of low."

Bad Tiger looked her right back in the eye. "You said yourself he wasn't going to get any better."

"*Without a doctor* he wasn't going to get any better," Jane said. "He shot him in cold blood."

"Buddy knew the score," Bad Tiger said as Timmy came back. "And I'll tell you, cutie pie, doctor or no doctor, he wasn't going to make it. I've seen it before. He had done mostly bled out. We done him a favor."

13

"We have to keep them all?" Timmy said. "How about I just shoot the girl, the blabbermouth."

I felt Jane grab my elbow.

"One hostage is good," Bad Tiger said, "but I reckon three is better. They get to be trouble, we'll bump them off. I'll let you start with Blabbermouth."

"You would make my day, you let me do that," Timmy said.

They put us down in the ditch, right under our car, so that if it slid back, we'd be crushed like bugs. I guess this was their way of keeping us in line. It was scary, but I couldn't think about nothing but how Timmy shot Buddy like he was popping a bottle off a fence post. It hadn't meant no more to him than that. And I couldn't stop thinking about how Buddy knew it was coming. I wasn't even sure he minded all that much.

After Timmy killed Buddy, he looked in the turtle hull of the Buick, and I could tell from the way he was looking it wasn't his car. It was a car they had stole. Just like they was planning to steal ours. Whatever he was hoping to find wasn't there.

They looked in the hull of our car and found the spare, some tools for changing the tire, and something that made them real happy: about twelve feet of chain.

"They even got a toolbox in here," Bad Tiger said. "You folks was prepared."

I didn't say it wasn't our car and we didn't know the stuff was back there. It wouldn't have mattered.

Timmy walked back to the Buick and got behind the steering wheel. For a while I thought he might not get it started, but when he did, he drove it around in front of the Ford and kept it running while Bad Tiger fastened the chain to the rear bumper of the Buick and the front bumper of the Ford.

That's when they made us get down in the ditch.

"You better hope the chain don't have a weak link," Bad Tiger said, looking down on us in the ditch. "'Cause I want you to stay right there under the rear of it. That way you got something to think about in case the chain snaps or the Buick slips back into it."

We heard Bad Tiger get in behind the wheel of the Ford and start it up.

Jane said, "We could run now."

"Yeah," I said, "and we might get as far as climbing up the side of the ditch before we was popped. That Timmy, he can't wait to pop something. We're careful and wait for the right moment, we might get away."

"You're right," Jane said, and I felt those weren't words she used often. "But it isn't just Timmy. Buddy said Bad Tiger is even worse, and considering he knew him better than us, I'm going to take him at his word."

"They're both crazy," Tony said. "It don't matter which one is crazier than the other. It ain't no contest."

Jane patted him on the shoulder lightly. "That's a good point, Tony. A real good point."

We heard Big Tiger speak loudly. "All right. I got it in neutral. Pull."

"I just hope the chain don't slip," Jane said as the Ford rocked back and then moved forward.

In the next moment, they had it out of the ditch. Bad Tiger came around and looked down on us.

"Just stay where you are while we change the tire," he said.

They changed it and called us up, and we climbed out of the ditch. Bad Tiger took our little bags of goods and chucked them in the hull of the car and closed the lid without even looking in them.

"Now," Bad Tiger said, "this is how this is going to work. I'm going to drive for a while, and, girlie, you're gonna ride up front with me so Timmy won't decide to shoot you just for the heck of it. You two boys are going to ride on either side of

Timmy in the backseat. And don't get you no tough-guy ideas. You try to take him on, I can tell you now he's stronger than he looks. And you still got me. I have to pull the car over for any kind of trouble from any one of you, you all get left beside the road, and not so you can thumb a ride. You understand me?"

We said we did.

"That's good. That's real good. That way things will go smooth and there won't be any rough moments. We don't want any rough moments, now, do we?"

We agreed rough moments were not good.

"All right now," he said. "Just the way I told you, get in the car."

14

We rode in the car in the way Bad Tiger said for us to ride, and we rode that way all through the day and into the night, except for when they stopped to switch drivers, or we took turns going off in the woods one at a time to do our business.

When Timmy drove, Bad Tiger moved me up front with

Timmy, and he moved Jane to the backseat and sat between her and Tony. I don't think he did it because he cared all that much for Jane's welfare, I think it was because he admired Jane for standing up to them and kicking Timmy. I think he liked that, but it was nothing you could confuse for friendship.

At one point Timmy said, "The gas is almost gone."

"How much you got?" Bad Tiger said.

"Less than a quarter."

"All right, then. Let's stop for the night somewhere, and tomorrow we'll get some gas. We ought to be over the Texas line tomorrow. There's a couple little towns the way we're going. We'll stop in one of them."

Timmy had a new toothpick in his mouth, and I could see it in the glow from the lights on the instrument panel. He moved it from one side of his mouth to the other like the pendulum of a clock.

After a little bit, Timmy found a dirt road that wound up into some trees. He drove off the road and over what had once been a cow trail, but now there was no grass for cows. The trees weren't like the trees before, when we had found the green spot down by the big creek. They were like the ones closer to home, and I figured it was because here the soil had been farmed out, and the wind had come and blown it off the earth and shot it through the trees like bullets. The sand had torn off what leaves were left that hadn't been eaten by starving bugs and animals. Even the bark on the trees was beat off by the sand in spots, like the trees had been in terrible knife fights with one another.

We parked and they had us get out. The wind was cool.

The shadows wound and fell and twisted through the barren trees.

Bad Tiger stretched and looked around. "We'll be in Texas pretty soon," he said. "It don't look much better than Oklahoma."

"There's East Texas," Timmy said.

"Yeah, well, East Texas is all right. I like all those trees, creeks, and rivers."

"They got alligators down there, just like in Louisiana," Timmy said.

"Yeah," Bad Tiger said, "thanks for the nature tip. I know that. I got relatives from there. Or did once. They all died, and I shot my daddy, so I don't have any relatives anymore."

"You killed him?" Tony said.

"Last time I looked at him," Bad Tiger said, "he was still dead."

"You shot and killed your own pa?" Tony said.

"Me and him didn't get along," Bad Tiger said.

"An understatement, I'm sure," Jane said. "I didn't like my pa neither, but I didn't shoot him. Course, we left him under a tractor and some dirt."

Bad Tiger laughed. "You're all right, girlie. I bet if someone dipped you in hot water you'd come out pink and cute. Fixed your hair, put a nice dress on you, you'd look all right."

"You don't worry none about my looks," Jane said.

Bad Tiger laughed. He said, "You kids go over and sit down by that tree there, and don't get any ideas. I'll get mad if you do, and if you make me run after you, you can't imagine how mad I'll be."

Actually, I could imagine.

We went over and put our backs against the tree. I couldn't tell what kind of tree it was in the dark, but it felt good to be sitting there with my back against it, away from Bad Tiger and Timmy.

I looked around for anything that might be a place to hide if we did make a break for it, but that little clutch of trees we were in was it. There was a rise of land that hid us from the main road, and that was some distance off anyway. The moon was high and partial, but bright. It wasn't a great night for trying to make a run for it.

"I think they circled back up to the Dust Bowl," Jane said. She said it so only we could hear. "The scenery changed for the better for a while, and now it's like it was when we left. I think they're running the roads in a way they think they can avoid the law."

"They took a lot of back roads, all right," I said. "Some main ones, like the one we just come off of, but a lot of back roads."

"They're zigzagging to Texas," Jane said. "If they're even going to Texas. I think all that talk might have been for our benefit so if we got away, we wouldn't know what they had in mind."

"Yeah," I said. "I think we're still high up in Oklahoma. They've turned us around and confused us so we wouldn't know it."

"I know it," Jane said.

"Yes, of course—how could you not, being all-knowing? I just wish you'd been all-knowing before that tire blew so we could have pulled off and changed it before our friends came up."

"Oh, give it a rest."

I did. We sat in silence for a long time until Tony said, "Did you see the way Timmy shot Buddy?"

"I don't think it meant a thing to him," Jane said. "Maybe he saw it like putting an animal out of its misery, but I don't think so. I think he wanted to do it just so he could kill something. I know people like that. Boys, I'll have to add. They kill birds that don't hurt nothing and that they don't eat. They kill them and pick them up and look at them and toss them, then they kill another. They don't do it for no other reason than the pleasure of the kill. That's the kind of men these are."

"I'm so scared," Tony said.

He sounded like he was about to break out bawling.

"Don't cry," Jane said. "Don't give them that. Don't you cry, you hear?"

"Yeah," he said, choking back a sob. "I hear you."

"We'll just have to wait for our moment," I said.

"That's right," Jane said. "Our moment. And it'll come."

"Way I figure, a moment don't always come," Tony said.

"Sure it will," Jane said. "We'll get our moment. It'll come when we least expect it, and we got to be ready to take advantage of it. It'll come."

"If they don't kill us first," Tony said.

"Don't talk like that," Jane said. "You can't think like that. It's defeatist. Think of John Carter of Mars. You remember those books? I read them to you, remember."

Tony nodded. "I remember."

"What was John Carter of Mars's slogan?"

"I still live."

"That's right. We'll be fine. We got to watch for our moment is all. We got to play it smart. We still live."

15

What they did was they took turns watching us, sitting with their backs against a tree directly across from us, wearing their guns. The night had grown cool. Bad Tiger had his gun on now and his coat, and when I was last aware of one of them on guard, just before I fell asleep, it was him, sitting at the base of a tree across the way looking at us.

Sometime in the night I woke up, but I didn't open my eyes at first. I just laid there and listened to Jane breathe. She had fallen asleep, and her head had ended up on my shoulder. I could smell her hair. All she had gone through, and she still smelled good. I felt kind of funny, but it was a good kind of funny, and even under the circumstances, it cheered me up a little. My shoulder hurt from the weight of her head, but I didn't want to do anything to disturb her.

Tony had laid out on the ground in front of us. He had his arm in such a way he could lay his noggin on it. He was sleeping deeply. I could hear his steady breathing.

I looked to see whose shift it was, but there was no one sitting beneath the tree across the way. I moved my eyes without moving my head, saw that both Bad Tiger and Timmy had given up on the guard business and had built a little fire under a tree not too far from the car. It was a cool night, and though I wasn't miserable, the idea of that fire seemed like a good thing. Not that I was in any frame of mind to get up and go over there and join them.

They were talking softly, but their voices still carried on the night, and I could understand every word. They were talking about somebody called Strangler.

"He took us for a ride," Timmy said.

"Yeah, well, the ride ain't over," Bad Tiger said.

"He took all the money and run out on us, and he's good and gone. I'd call that ride over."

"He shouldn't do a thing like that to Bad Tiger," Bad Tiger said of himself. "He ought not to have thought he could get away with a thing like that."

"He did get away with it."

"Keep talking like that," Bad Tiger said, "and you'll be laid out under one of these trees like Buddy."

"I didn't mean nothing by it. I'm just saying."

"And I'm just saying I'm going to catch up with him, and when I do, I wouldn't want to be Strangler Nugowski. And here's another thing. That fifty thousand we got. That's the biggest haul I ever took. That bank must have had every payroll there was in it. Splitting that four ways, that was good money. With Buddy hit like he was, I figured it'd be three ways at some point. But then Strangler run off with the money."

"Which made it a one-way split," Timmy said.

"Yeah, but we get it back, it's a two-way split, and that's good. He won't be splitting nothing, but you and me, we'll take it right down the middle."

"Unless he's spent it."

"He hasn't spent fifty thousand dollars. A few bucks here and there, but he hasn't spent it yet. You know what he's going to do, don't you?"

"I got an idea."

"Yeah," Bad Tiger said, "and if you're smart, you got the same idea I got."

"The kid."

"Yeah, the kid. He thinks he can take that money and use it to get his kid's foot fixed."

"I remember—twisted up or something."

"Clubfooted. They can fix that sometimes, and he wants it fixed. So to get it fixed, he's got to go back and find her."

"East Texas," Timmy said.

"Tyler. I been there. I know where it is. He'll probably show up there. He goes where he knows. I know that much about him. Eventually, he'll be there."

"Way we're going, we ain't never going to get there."

"Take a straight shot, we might not get there either. Cops

are all over the place. I figure we'll run into some at some point, and we do, we got those kids for hostages."

"What happens when we get to East Texas?" Timmy asked.

"We find Strangler and we get the money."

"I mean with the kids."

"Oh," Bad Tiger said. "I don't know. We could let them go, or you could shoot them. But you know, I'm thinking about keeping the girl."

"You've gone silly."

"She's a looker."

"There's lots of lookers," Timmy said.

"They don't look like that. I just want to clean her up and get some war paint on her, have her hair fixed, some nice clothes, keep her around for a while."

"I know what you want. I don't have to puzzle over what you want. I know."

"Yeah, well, you're right," Bad Tiger said.

"She ain't nothing but a kid."

"You sure are standing up for her. A while ago you were a man wanted to shoot her," Bad Tiger said.

"Not exactly standing up for her, but I know if you take a shine to her, I don't get to shoot her. And I owe her one."

Bad Tiger laughed. "She sure laid one into you, didn't she?"

"It's not so funny from this end."

"Yeah, but from my end it's a riot," Bad Tiger said. "You know what I think?"

"What?"

"I think you'd like to see her cleaned up too, spend a little time with her before you shoot her. How's that thinking?"

"It's a thought that might have crossed my mind, but I don't have to like her to want that. And for me, she don't even have to be cleaned up. So, yeah. It crossed my mind."

"Well, uncross the thought," Bad Tiger said. "She stays with anyone any time at all, it's me."

16

Of course I had been thinking about getting away, but now, it was all I could think about. The idea that Bad Tiger and Timmy might do something to Jane was more than I could stand, and just a day or two ago, I wasn't even sure I liked her.

She was a liar and a thief and a bit of a con, and she had dragged me into this business with her and her little brother, and I wasn't even sure where I was going or why. There was just something about her that made you want to follow her. Some kind of thing that made you feel she knew where she was going, and you ought to want to go too.

I didn't feel so good about it now. It had been bad enough at home with my folks dead and buried in the barn, but now I was on the run, and we was with real gangsters. Heck, they had stole the car that we had stole from a dead man, so we couldn't exactly place ourselves on a much higher level than they were. Course, we hadn't shot anybody, and they had. But to tell you true, I wasn't feeling so good about myself right then.

Bottom line was, they had guns and bad attitudes, and they both wanted Jane for one thing or another, and none of it good. On top of that, one of their partners, a guy called Strangler, seemed to have betrayed them to take the money to get some kind of doctoring for his kid, and they were going after him, and if the law showed up, we were hostages. And there wasn't any guarantee that the cops would be all that worried about our safety. We might get shot at from both sides.

I thought on things awhile, decided there was nothing to be done at the moment. And Jane had been right about them driving back up into the Dust Bowl. They were zigzagging, but doing it in such a way it would eventually take them southeast, into Texas.

I closed my eyes and surprised myself by going to sleep, only waking up when Timmy put a foot in my side.

"Up and at it," he said. "We're moving out."

"I'm hungry," Tony said.

"Get up," Timmy said.

"What about breakfast?" Jane said.

"What about it?" Timmy said. "Was you expecting it in bed?"

68

"That would be nice," she said.

Timmy kicked her. I grabbed his leg and lifted it and he fell back on his butt. I was up and on him then, but when I straddled him and drew back my fist, he pulled out the automatic and put it against the tip of my nose.

"Why don't you go on and do that," he said. "See how it works out for you."

Next thing I felt was being pulled off him. It was Bad Tiger. He jerked me to my feet and slapped me hard enough it knocked me down and made my ears ring.

"I ain't up for it," Bad Tiger said. "Not even a little bit. Everybody get in the car. Now! Timmy, you're driving."

17

I sat up front with Timmy at the wheel. We hadn't gone far before he turned on the radio, but all he got was a sound like someone rubbing a jagged rock over sandpaper. He turned it off and hummed a little, whistled a few bars, then went silent.

I started trying to pay attention to things. I had grown up

on a farm and I knew weather, but on direction I could be iffy. I was never like Daddy, who could get up in the middle of the night and be spun around and still point true north. He always knew which direction was which, and he could tell time by the sun, and there were times when he wasn't in sight of the sun and he could still tell you what time it was within five to ten minutes. He could hear a dog run across the yard in the middle of the night. But I never really picked up his skills. Heck, maybe they couldn't be taught. Maybe they were inborn and I just didn't have them.

I watched out the window to see if I could locate the sun, but it wasn't high up yet. There was a lot of light from one direction, and since it was early, it stood to reason that was the east. That was where the sun rose on its way to the middle of the sky, and then down on the other side into darkness.

Okay, I decided, we were finally traveling south, because the sun's strongest light and the warmest spot was on my left shoulder, and the shadow from the steering wheel lay across me. Yes, to the left of me was east, to my right was west, and that meant we were heading south, and into Texas.

I was just sitting there with my mind on that, when Timmy said, "You ever cut up anything alive with a knife, boy?"

I glanced at him.

"No," I said.

He grinned. "It's an experience."

He went back to driving, fished a toothpick out of his shirt pocket, and put it in his mouth. "It's going to be a hot one," he said. "I wish I hadn't lost my hat. I'd like it better with my hat. It gets hot, a hat keeps the sun off, but mostly I'm just used to wearing it."

"Shut up about your hat," Bad Tiger said. "Just shut up and drive."

I glanced at Timmy. He swallowed heavily, like what he was choking down was a green chicken gizzard full of bile.

We come to a little town with a filling station. We was still in Oklahoma, because painted on the buildings were signs with the town's name and *Oklahoma* on the end of it. I didn't point this out to Bad Tiger and Timmy, and I hoped Jane wouldn't. It was all right we knew they were lying the night before, but it wasn't a good idea to let them know we knew.

When we were parked in front of the station, they pulled at their coats so their guns were well hid, and Bad Tiger said, "Any of you talk, it better be something you've always wanted to say, 'cause it's going to be your last bit of chat. Timmy, you stand outside with him till he puts in the gas. Then go in and get us something to eat, some Coca-Colas."

"Some tissues or some toilet paper would be nice," Jane said.

"Those are your last words?" Big Tiger said.

"Nobody's come out yet," she said.

Bad Tiger grinned. "You like to push it, don't you?"

Timmy slammed a fist down on the horn. It made me jump. Timmy looked at me and laughed.

"Nervous?"

About then a young man in coveralls strolled out from behind the station and Timmy started to get out of the car. Bad Tiger said, "And don't forget the toilet paper, they got any. They don't, get some paper towels. The lady here, she likes it tidy."

71

Timmy got out of the car and told the station man to fill it up.

When it was full, the boy checked under the hood and checked the tires, and then he and Timmy went inside the station.

After a while I heard a pop, and Timmy came out of the station with a bag of groceries. He put them on the seat between us and started the car.

Bad Tiger said, "You didn't need to do that. It just makes it hotter for us."

"How was I going to pay for it? My good looks?"

"You didn't have to shoot him," Bad Tiger said.

"You said that," Timmy said, pulling onto the road. "But if it makes you feel better, I just shot him in the foot. He ain't going to go tell anyone anything quick-like. And he ain't got no phone in there. I asked if I could borrow it, just to see. That gunshot, it didn't sound like nothing. We're off scotfree. At least enough to get us down the road a ways."

"Yeah, well," Bad Tiger said. "You better hope so."

18

By the time we pulled off the road it was near dark, and I was feeling sick from hunger. They found a place down by a little creek that had some water in it, and we got the groceries out.

Timmy used the car door handle to hook the Coca-Cola bottles under so he could pop off the lids. It scarred the car. It wasn't my car, but it made me feel guilty. Old Man Turpin had always taken care of it, and now it was scarred. He'd had it for a while and kept it perfect, and in a couple of minutes, Timmy had messed it up.

There weren't any trees right where we were, but the bank was deep and the water was shallow, running over white gravel that we could see in the creek bed through the water. I looked down the creek a ways, and about thirty feet away was a little clutch of struggling willows growing on the edge of the bank. The bank had fallen out beneath them, leaving their roots hanging down like electrical wires. The place where the dirt had washed away was from a long time ago, when there had been some good rains and the water had been high and had pushed the earth out. The dirt there had turned hard and it was dark, unlike the sand along the creek, which was red and white mixed up together the way I thought strawberry and vanilla ice cream might look.

Truth was, I'd only seen pictures of strawberry ice cream. Only kind I had ever had was vanilla, made with ice cream salt and milk and lots of arm cranking on the ice cream maker. Someday, I wanted to try strawberry. It was another thing to live for, and another reason to think about escaping.

Timmy took a pocketknife and opened up some cans of potted meat with it and gave them to us. That made me remember I still had a pocketknife. They hadn't even bothered to search us. It wasn't much, that knife, but I liked knowing I had it. I had forgotten all about it.

We sat and scooped the meat out of the cans with our fingers and licked it off and drank our Coca-Colas. When I finished, I was still hungry, but I was used to that. There never seemed to be enough. The last time I had really been full was when I had eaten all that rabbit, and that had been the first time in a long time.

Timmy went back to the car and came back carrying some toilet paper. He come close to Jane and threw it hard, hitting her in the head.

He laughed when she let out a noise.

"How you like that?"

Jane picked up the paper and laid it in her lap. She said, "Don't think I'll forget that."

"Ha," Timmy said. "Do or don't. I'd rather you didn't."

Timmy went over to the sack and pulled out a couple

extra cans of potted meat. He tossed one to Bad Tiger and kept one for himself. They opened them with their pocketknives and ate.

There was a darkness moving in from the north, and I was proud of the fact that I was now certain which way was which. I was learning. At first they just looked like rain clouds, but I'd seen clouds like that too many times. I knew better.

Bad Tiger had seen them too. He said, "Looks like tonight we're going to have a blow. I figure me and Timmy will sleep in the car. And I'll keep you with us, sister."

"Why me?" she said.

"Why not you?" Bad Tiger said. "I got to have one of you in the car so the other two don't run off. You're my hostage to hold the other hostages, so to speak. Course, they still might run off. But if they do, I still got you, and me and you, we could get cozy if we had to."

"I'd rather die," Jane said.

"Yeah, that could happen," Timmy said.

"You don't want to value yourself too highly," Bad Tiger said. "'Cause a thing you ought to know is we don't even value ourselves all that much."

"I hate to admit it," Jane said, "but that does show something I didn't expect about the two of you."

"What's that, sister?" Bad Tiger said.

"You're good judges of character," she said.

Bad Tiger let out a hoot and Timmy sat silent.

"We got some time before the storm," Bad Tiger said, "so you got some business to take care of in the bushes, this is the

75

time to do it. You got your paper, now, honey. That make you happy?"

"Ecstatic," said Jane.

19

It wasn't long before I realized the clouds coming our way were moving fast, and much too fast for a storm front, even if it had been a tornado coming.

And it wasn't true clouds at all. I figured that when they came so fast and when I heard the loud hum. I knew then it was grasshoppers, millions of them. I had seen clouds like this before, several times, and I hadn't liked it then, and I didn't like it now.

The humming blackness came down from the sky and hit the willows down below, and in a moment the grasshoppers ate the green off of them, and the willows shook like they was in a high wind, but the only wind was the wind the grass-hoppers made.

"Hit the dirt!" I yelled, and me and Jane and Tony

dropped down over the side of the bank. But I didn't go down before I saw Bad Tiger running like a frightened little girl toward the Ford, and Timmy on his tail.

The hoppers hit me hard, so hard and in such a big wave, it was like being kicked by a mule. Even if I hadn't been diving for the ground, they would have knocked me down anyway. They splattered against me and I swear I was lifted forward a bit as they hit and I dove.

I lay with my face down tight against the bank and I could feel them crawling all over me, tugging at my shirt. I lifted my head a little. The sky was dark with them. So dark, it seemed like early evening.

I saw Jane and Tony. They were both down close to the water.

I said, "Crawl," and a grasshopper hit my mouth. It tasted sour. I spat it out and started crawling, and when I looked back, Jane and Tony were crawling with me.

We crawled along the bank and still the grasshoppers came. We crawled into them instead of away from them, and finally we came to where the dirt had been scooped out by wind and rain and time, underneath the willows. When we got there, I saw that the indention was deeper than I'd expected. You couldn't tell that from where we had been, but once you were right up on it, you could see it was almost a cave. And down low there was an even deeper opening. Roots dangled down like worms. I could see all the way through the lower opening. It wasn't very wide, but it went deep and it came out after a great distance. There was water in the groove. It was the water that kept it open like this.

When rain was hard and the water was high, it must have churned through there like it was shot out of a hose.

I crawled in and Jane and Tony crawled after me. We kept crawling toward what little light we could see on the other side. Behind us the dark shadow of the grasshoppers covered the ground.

We crawled for a long ways, and it was tight in there. I feared for a moment I was going to get stuck. But I made it. A water snake was swimming briskly in front of me, heading for the light. It wasn't a poisonous snake, but it gave me the willies nonetheless.

I dug in with my elbows and kept my head down and kept going. The light was getting brighter. It was tight now on the sides and at the top. I couldn't turn my head anymore and look back. The roots were starting to catch in my hair, but I kept moving. My hair got snapped out of my head by the roots as I crawled.

Finally I came to where the light was, and the hole was very small there. I laid with my face turned to keep my nose out of the little bit of water and pushed on through, breaking some of the ground apart as I did. I came out on the other side and rolled down a sandy hill and into a wind-made ditch.

I crawled up the side of the hill and took a look. I could see the Ford. It was covered in grasshoppers.

It was like where we were was the line. Everything on the other side of the ditch was grasshoppers. On this side was just us.

"Now's our chance," I said.

Ducking low, we ran away from the ditch, away from the

Ford and all the grasshoppers, away from Timmy and Bad Tiger.

We went swiftly across a large field. Then we came to the main road and crossed over that, went down a small ridge of dirt, then moved toward a cluster of trees that had long ago been hit by sand and grasshoppers. There was nothing for the grasshoppers to like anymore. They had left nothing. Like so many trees around here, they was just big dry sticks.

The tree trunks were pretty big, though, so we got behind those for a second, dropping down on our knees and looking back across the way as we got our breath.

The grasshoppers had turned slightly and were moving across the sky like a giant wiggling snake, and now there were more than before, and everything was dark and thick with them. I figured pretty soon they would be smashing into the trees where we were, into us.

It was then that Jane said, "Jack. They've eaten off the back of your shirt."

I took off my shirt and just had on my dirty undershirt. The back of my shirt was split open in a jagged way. The grasshoppers had eaten a large stretch of cotton out of it.

Jane laughed. She held up her hand. She was still clutching the toilet paper. It was dirty and wet, but she still had it.

I said, "Turn around."

She did. The back of her pants had been bitten out by the bugs and I could see her underthings. I told her.

"Oh no. Give me your shirt."

I gave it to her, and she tied it around her waist so what was left of my shirt covered her rear end.

We turned Tony around and gave him a look. They hadn't hit him at all.

"How about that," I said. "Our moment came."

"Well, it's only a moment," Jane said. "So we got to hustle away from here, and fast."

20

Walking along through what had once been farmland but was now nothing but sand, we came to an old barn that was mostly fallen down. The sky was clear, and night was setting in, and the stars were bright. We didn't know if Bad Tiger and Timmy were still looking for us, but we stayed away from the road.

Earlier, we thought we heard the Ford's big engine whining along up over the rise, on the main road. Going first one way, then the other. We heard a door slam, and I thought I could hear men talking. I didn't know for sure that it was Bad Tiger and Timmy, but I wasn't interested enough to go up there and find out.

The barn was way off from the road, and it had three good sides and most of a roof. We went inside. There was an old sand-covered tarp in there, and we scraped the sand off with our feet, which took some time; then we took the tarp out into the open air and shook it and snapped the dust off of it.

Carrying the tarp back inside, we laid it out on the sand and pushed it down with our hands and knees and found us a place to lie down. It was the best bed I had been on in a while.

As we lay there, I told them about Strangler Nugowski. I told them what he had done and that he was probably in Tyler, Texas, and Bad Tiger and Timmy were going after him.

"Why didn't you tell us before?" asked Jane.

"When? During the grasshopper storm, or while we was sleeping last night?" I said. "I ain't exactly had the time for an in-depth conversation."

"All right," Jane said, "you can slide by on that one.

"Strangler?" Jane said. "Really? Is that what his mother named him? 'Come on in to supper, Strangler. Come on in and wash your hands and I'll let you strangle one of the chickens for us to eat. Course, you have to wash your hands again.'"

"I kind of doubt his given name is Strangler," I said.

"I'd like to see his birth certificate," Jane said. "I think it would be funny if his mama named him Strangler and it says so right there on the paper."

I laughed that time. It wasn't that funny, but I was tired and everything seemed kind of amusing right then.

"I don't know," Tony said. "I wish my name was something like that. I wouldn't mind being called Crusher."

"Go on to sleep, Crusher," I said.

"That poor man," Jane said. "Them going after him and all."

"He stole money too," I said. "And he might have shot someone. He might have shot Buddy."

"But him taking the money to fix his daughter's foot," she said. "That's sweet."

"I suppose," I said.

"Maybe y'all could call me Crusher from now on," Tony said.

"No," me and Jane said together.

"We are not going to call you Crusher," Jane said. "Tony is a perfectly good name."

"It sounds sissy to me," Tony said.

"It's fine," Jane said. "Tell him, Jack."

"It's fine," I said.

"You say that 'cause you're sweet on her," Tony said.

"I am not," I said.

"Oh, come on," Jane said. "You are too."

"I'm not."

"Yes you are. You let me put my head on your shoulder all night."

"I was just being nice," I said.

"Sure you were," Jane said.

"Well, you're the one put your head on my shoulder," I said.

"It was better than the hard ground or that tree trunk," she said.

I didn't have anything to say to that. I was still trying to think of a snappy comeback when Jane said, "I still got the toilet paper anyone needs it. It's mostly dry, and you can peel off a couple layers you need to go."

Neither Tony or me answered. I could hear Tony already breathing evenly in deep sleep.

Jane said softly, "We still live."

Next thing I knew, it was morning.

21

In the morning we brushed ourselves off as best we could and walked up to the road and looked around carefully. We didn't see Bad Tiger, Timmy, or the Ford.

I couldn't imagine them hanging around. They didn't want us so bad they'd chance being found by the law, or so I thought. Still, we stayed cautious.

We posted a lookout at the edge of the road behind a tree, and the idea was to switch from time to time, until we saw a car or truck coming that we thought might give us a ride.

I hadn't been on duty more than a few minutes, when I

looked up the road and saw a truck with panel boards on the back moving toward us.

I whistled up Jane and Tony. They came running. I went to the side of the road and put a thumb out. Jane and Tony were soon standing beside me, doing the same.

The truck stopped. It was a man who might have been younger than he looked, 'cause his teeth were missing and his clothes were worn and he hadn't shaved in a few days, and his skin had burned the color of dried blood.

He stuck his head out the window, said, "You're going my way, you can ride. But there's hogs in the back. The girl can sit up here if she likes."

"I like," Jane said, then went around in front of the truck and got in on the passenger's side.

Me and Tony went around back and climbed over the boards and eased ourselves inside the truck bed with a half dozen small black and white hogs and a piglet. There was hog mess on the floor and it stunk.

We clung to the wood slats and the man drove us out of there. It was better when we got to moving, because the wind blew some of the stink away, and it felt good because it was starting to turn off hot.

I could see through the back window that Jane was chatting the driver up, maybe telling him how we were a talented bunch of singers on our way to make our fortune with our family in East Texas. Or maybe it was some other lie. Anyway, she was talking a lot, and he was nodding and grinning.

We rode into a little town where everything seemed to

be either gray or orange. Once, the buildings had been brightly painted, but the sandstorms had sanded them down and made them bleaker. The orange was the color that was left after all the paint had been worked over by sand. Before the sand, it could have been red or yellow.

We were let off in front of the general store. We had lost our bags of goods, but Jane still had the money she had saved stuffed in her pocket, and I still had my pocketknife, so we weren't without something.

In the store we looked around for a box of crackers and had the counterman cut us off a chunk of rat cheese and some bologna and we bought some bread by the slice. We got a half dozen Coca-Colas and a few penny candies.

The counterman wrapped up the bread and meat and cheese in separate pieces of wax paper, and then he wrapped it all up in brown paper. Jane paid for it. He put it all in a grocery bag, except the Coca-Colas, and he put those in a double bag so where they were damp from the cooler they wouldn't wet through the sack.

A nice-looking woman standing behind us in line, said, "What have you children been doing? You smell like hogs."

"We're pretty near out of money," Jane said. "In fact, what we just spent is about it. Those two got that stench from cleaning out a man's hogpens with shovels. I did the wash for him too. He paid us mostly in food and a night's sleep, but a bath is something we haven't had. And truthfully, if anyone ever needed it, it's those two."

"You don't even have a shirt?" the woman said to me.

"I started not to let him in the store dressed like that," said the counterman, "wearing that dirty undershirt, but I figured it wasn't by choice."

"No, it wasn't," Jane said. "We been hitchhiking for a week on account of our parents just dropped us off on the side of the road. Us and our old yellow dog. They told us we was going to stop and pick flowers, 'cause our grandparents were buried up this way. But that was a lie. They drove off and left us when we was out picking."

"I ain't seen a flower around here in a month of Sundays," the counterman said. "The storms have knocked them all down."

"There were just three or four, actually," Jane said. "You don't expect your folks to do a thing like that. Lie to you about your grandparents' graves, and there being flowers, and then them just driving off and leaving us. It wasn't something we expected."

"What happened to the dog?" the lady asked.

"Hit by a truck," Jane said. "Happened pretty quick. Merciful, really, otherwise he would have starved to death, and we might even have had to eat him. Our parents never named him for just that reason. They said you shouldn't name something you might have to eat. They used to joke that they wasn't sure they was going to name us."

"That's awful," said the lady.

"Isn't it?" Jane said.

"Beside the road?" the woman said. "Well, my goodness. And your dog run over too."

"It was pretty sad," Jane said, "but I've tried to keep us

together and not let these two get in any trouble. We had to rent Jack here out to a man we come across, for . . . well, who knows what."

"You poor child," the woman said, and put her hand on my head. She pulled it back pretty quick, though. My hair was full of grasshopper guts, grit, and pig stink.

"You rented your brother out?" the counterman said. "You rented him?"

"Hunger is not a great bearer of judgment," Jane said.

"That sounds like a cock-and-bull story to me," said the counterman.

"Oh, don't say that," said the lady. "You kids come with me. I'll see you get a real meal. We'll put those things of yours in the icebox. You can get a bath, and tomorrow I'll talk to my church friends, and maybe we can find you a home. We've done a lot for orphans."

"Thank you," said Jane. "It's good to know that Christian charity still exists in this world. I, for one, had come to doubt it."

The woman said, "Come on," and started leading us out the door.

I hadn't taken a step, though, when the counterman reached across the counter and got me by the elbow.

"Hey, now. Mrs. Carson is a good widow lady. Don't you kids go and take advantage of her."

I looked up and saw Jane and Tony and the lady were near the door.

"We've had a hard time of it," I said.

"I don't believe a word of it," he said.

"You think that's something," I said, "you ought to hear the truth."

I pulled loose of him and followed them outside.

22

It was night and it was cool, and me and Jane were sitting in Mrs. Carson's porch swing. Tony was inside at the table eating a large piece of chocolate cake. His third.

I could turn in the swing and look through the window and see him in there. Mrs. Carson was fussing over him, pouring him up a glass of milk. When she finished doing that, she sat down to talk to him. She really had taken a shine to Tony.

We were all clean, having bathed and washed our hair. We had been given clothes that Mrs. Carson had gotten from some of her church friends. Now me and Jane had cups of hot cocoa and were sitting in the swing, moving it slightly with our feet.

It felt good to be clean, but it didn't feel good to have hoodwinked that poor lady.

"Mrs. Carson must be rich," Jane said.

"You really had to say I was hired out like that?"

"It just come to me."

"The man in the store didn't believe a word of it. And you had to add in a dog?"

"It wasn't as crazy as what really happened. Picked up by gangsters, saw a man shot, and then we snuck off in a grasshopper storm."

"You forgot stealing a car from a dead man," I said. "And leaving your father under his tractor and a pile of sand."

"Me and him never did get along."

"That's still not a good reason to leave him under a tractor," I said.

"It is sad," she said, "but I didn't have a family like yours. They loved you."

"Daddy could have loved me better," I said. "He hung himself and left me to fend for things."

"Yeah, that wasn't good."

"But I'll tell you, Jane. I think about them at least once every hour of every day."

"I know you mean that symbolically," she said, "because you don't have a watch."

I grinned at her. Sometimes with Jane, it was all you could do.

"Well, I think about them a lot. And it is every day. At first, I kept thinking about Daddy hanging and Mama dead in her bed. But now I don't think about that so much. I think about the good times, and there was plenty. If Mama hadn't got sick, everything would have been okay."

"If there hadn't been sandstorms, she wouldn't have been sick," Jane said. "There hadn't been a dust bowl and grasshoppers and the like, we'd all be fine. Well, almost. Like I said, I was planning on leaving from the time I knew there was a way out. I was going to go just as soon as I could. Pa going down under that tractor was just the straw that broke the camel's back. I wanted to be anywhere but where we was."

"If Mama and Daddy had been all right," I said, "I could have stayed."

"Yeah, well," Jane said. "Everyone's not made the same."

She turned and looked back through the window behind the swing. "Tony looks happy," she said.

"Yeah," I said.

"I was wondering if he should stay."

"I take it we aren't?" I said.

"Of course not. Mrs. Carson gets to thinking about that story, and that store man tells her he doesn't believe it, and we have to back it up somehow, we're cooked. But Tony, I think he could stay and they wouldn't care about the lie."

"He won't stay," I said. "He'll go with you."

"Maybe."

"Where exactly are we going, anyway?" I said.

"I figured that was clear," she said.

"Not to me."

"We can't let Strangler get killed on account of he stole money to help his kid."

"We can't?"

90

"We shouldn't. Strangler being a father like that, he's more than mine was. Pa wouldn't have done nothing to make things bad for us, but if I needed an operation for something, I'd have had to cut on myself with a butter knife and patch it all up with flour paste and a roll of electrician's tape. He'd have called it God's will, me coming down with some problem or the other."

"It's really none of our business," I said. "Strangler has to tote his own water."

"I know that," Jane said. "But it doesn't hurt to warn him. I don't like Bad Tiger and Timmy."

"Of course you don't. If you did, I'd be worried."

"I didn't like what I thought they were thinking when it come to me."

"Ain't no thinking about it," I said. "That's exactly what they're thinking, only with a killing at the end of it all."

"Yeah, well, I told Timmy I wouldn't forget he hit me with that toilet paper."

"So that's what this is about," I said. "You getting even. You think helping Strangler gets you even with Timmy over a roll of tossed toilet paper?"

"Some. But I don't want some man's death on my hands who was just trying to help a crippled child neither."

"Strangler ain't your father. He might be as bad as they are. He might kill you himself."

"I don't think so. Not with him doing for his daughter what he did. Robbing a bank to pay for her operation. That's a fellow that's got backbone. That's love. . . . Besides, that's not all that matters. Doing something to help someone else that's between a rock and a hard place, it's just the sort of thing that gives you a sense of worth."

"Couldn't you find something else other than trying to keep Strangler from getting killed to give you worth?" I said. "We could turn out worthy but dead."

"I'm not asking you to do a thing," she said.

"The heck you aren't," I said. "I'd say you're asking me plenty."

"Jack, you don't have to do a thing you don't want to do. It's me I'm talking about. I want to do something that gives me adventure and does something noble for someone. Something that makes me want to get up and get going in the morning, not just lie there hoping the wind quits blowing. Life needs to be about something more than milking a cow or throwing corn at chickens. King Arthur and his knights weren't about milking cows and feeding chickens. They had quests to keep them busy."

"We're not King Arthur or his knights, and they weren't fooling with gangsters."

"You, Jack Catcher, are easily satisfied. Pa never figured anything for me but what he had. Getting married, and maybe having a husband that didn't run off, and me having babies between putting up canned goods and frying a chicken."

"Lots of people do that," I said. "They get along okay."

Jane nodded. "It's all right if they want it. But no one asked me what I wanted. Pa, everyone else, just expected me to do a certain thing because that's what they thought life was. I don't need some obligation to hold me down.

What I need is a choice that isn't already made for me. What I need is to go out and see if the world is flat, round, or some kind of triangle. I need to feel I've seen something and done something that isn't the same thing everyone else has seen or done."

We sat and listened to crickets for a while. I turned over in my head what she had been saying. It was more than I could get hold of.

I looked up, smiled at her. "Say, where is that toilet paper, anyway?"

"I left it in the pig truck," she said. "I figured he ought to have something for his troubles."

"It isn't much," I said, "but it was nice of you."

"Actually, I just forgot it."

We sat for a little while without talking. Finally I said, "Do you really want to try and find Strangler?"

"We need a mission," Jane said. "A goal. Like Sir Galahad. He went searching for the Holy Grail. Strangler will be our grail. The quest will teach us who we are."

"You have to teach someone that?" I asked.

"I think you do," Jane said. "And through the process of the quest, we learn what we're looking for. The quest is everything."

"What are we looking for?"

"I don't know," she said. "I reckon we'll know it when we find it."

"What's a quest, by the way?"

"Same as a mission. Same as a goal."

"Then why not say goal or mission?"

"Because it gives it weight to call it a quest," she said. "It gives it true purpose and meaning. It just sounds better."

"What about Tony? Maybe he don't want a mission. Maybe he wants to be like everyone else."

"I don't know about Tony. He's just a kid. I practically raised him. What with Mama running off with that Bible salesman—which, by the way, put me off church forever—and our pa not really caring if we was loved, just doing what he thought was responsible because it's what was responsible, I've been pretty much all the mother and father Tony's had."

"Being responsible isn't all bad," I said.

"Not all bad. But it sure means a lot more when you do it because you love somebody, and not because you think you're supposed to and the church wants you to, or your neighbors, or whoever. I just wanted to be loved like any daughter. And Tony ought to have been loved like any son. Not just loved by his big sister. You got some of that kind of feeling, Jack. I can tell. Your pa may have lost his place when your mama died, but he loved you. Mine didn't. Me and Tony was the same as property. We might as well have been middlebusters and cultivators for all the love Pa gave us."

"I don't know I had it so good," I said. "Daddy wrote me a suicide note."

"What did it say?"

I told her.

"There you go. At least there was an apology involved."

She leaned over close to me and said, "Look here."

I turned and she leaned forward and kissed me. I liked it. We did it again.

When I pulled back that time, I hardly had any breath.

I leaned forward for one more. Jane said, "No. That's enough. Don't make more of it than what it was. A kiss between friends."

"It was mighty friendly," I said. I moved toward her again, but she put a hand on my chest and gently pushed me back.

"Wouldn't do us any good if Mrs. Carson saw me kissing my brother, now, would it?"

"I ain't your brother," I said.

"Yeah, but Mrs. Carson don't know that. That story I told earlier, I figure they've already got us pegged as a pretty odd family, so we don't want to put fuel on the fire, now, do we?"

23

Mrs. Carson's house was big. She had a room for me and Tony to share, and she gave Jane her own. After we went to bed, Jane slipped into our room. We still had the electric light on, which, come to think of it, was the only kind of lights Mrs. Carson had. At home we had some electricity, but with the sandstorms blowing down wires, we mostly used kerosene and candles.

The bed was nice and there was no dust anywhere. The house had the best-sealed windows I had ever seen.

All I knew was it kept out the dust.

I thought that this wouldn't be such a bad place to stay, and we really were orphans, and maybe those church people Mrs. Carson talked about could help us out.

Anyway, Jane came in and said, "Mrs. Carson wants to see us all."

We went into the kitchen, where Mrs. Carson sat looking clean and nice under the electric light over the kitchen table. She had a trim face, and the bones stood up high in her cheeks and her eyes were bright, like she was always surprised about something. I guess she was older than Mama by some years, but she didn't look worn out the way Mama had. Mrs. Carson was soft and smooth-looking, and when she moved, you couldn't take your eyes off her. She had a manner about her that was like some kind of strange but beautiful bird. She fit perfectly in her beautiful house.

The light over the table didn't have a pull cord, like I was used to. None of the lights in the house had that. They all had switches. The light over the table was a big chandelier with lots of bulbs, and it made quite a glow. It was almost like being out in the yard at high noon. The walls were bright with paint and the floors were shiny with polish, and there wasn't any sand in the corners or up in the curtains. Right then, at that moment, it was the perfect place to be.

Mrs. Carson smiled at us as we came in and asked us to sit at the table. When we were all seated, she said, "That story you told me earlier. I just want you to know I didn't believe a word of it. Not literally, anyway. But I do believe you kids are in trouble, and anyone that would make up a whopper like that is either a con person or someone who needs help. I decided you were the latter, though, girl, you have a bit of the former in you."

"Why, thank you," Jane said, as if it was a compliment.

"I wasn't always well off," Mrs. Carson said. "My husband and I had some good fortune. Now he's gone. I try to help others when I can."

"I'm sorry I lied to you," Jane said.

"That's all right," Mrs. Carson said, "but you must never do it again."

"Yes, ma'am," Jane said.

"The part about the dog was especially precious, dear," Mrs. Carson said. "But you must not butter up your stories so. It makes them too slippery to handle. And Jack here, I doubt that happened to him . . . what you said happened."

"No, ma'am, and he isn't my brother either."

"I didn't think so. You don't look anything alike. But Tony here, he's your brother, right?"

"Yes, ma'am," Jane said.

"What I want to tell you is this. If you want to stay, you can stay. I'll do what I can. I'm all alone, and I don't have any family. I wouldn't mind the company."

"I don't think we can," I said. "Jane and I have someone we want to help."

"Help?" Mrs. Carson said.

"It's a long story," I said, not wanting to tell her the truth, because it sounded almost as crazy as the story Jane had made up. "There isn't much to it. We just want to do right by someone."

"I hope that's the truth," Mrs. Carson said.

"It is, ma'am," Jane said.

Mrs. Carson nodded. "What about you, Tony?"

Tony looked at us, and then he looked at Mrs. Carson. "I like it here. I like it here fine," he said.

"Then you should stay," Jane said. "We'll come back. I will."

"Me too," I said.

"I'd like to stay, but I got to stick with my sister," Tony said. "She might need me."

Mrs. Carson nodded again. "I could get the law on you so you wouldn't go out there and get yourself hurt, but I haven't the heart for it. I wouldn't do that. You are welcome to stay as long as you like. And if you go away, you are welcome back. But with truer stories."

"When we come back," I said, "we will have the whole story for you. We appreciate your kindness. We really are orphans. We really have had bad times."

"Who hasn't?" Mrs. Carson said. "It's just the bad times aren't always the same kind of bad times for everybody."

24

We slept good that night knowing we weren't liars anymore, but we still got up early. I found some paper and a pencil in the kitchen and wrote a thank-you note to Mrs. Carson, and then we left quietly.

It was still dark when we started down the road. Mrs. Carson had given us some supplies, and we had those in big nice canvas bags slung over our shoulders. The bags were a little heavy, but as we ate what was in them, they would grow lighter. Not everything in them was food. There was a flashlight with spare batteries, some matches, and a few other odds and ends.

By the time the sun was up good, we were well out of town, and Jane, now wearing something nice, easily walked out to the edge of the road and caught us a ride by looking charming.

It was something she felt bad about in a way, as it didn't live up to her idea of women and equality. She had given me the lecture on it as we walked. I thought it made sense, though I wasn't sure I understood everything there was to know about it, and I'm not sure she did either.

The ride was another truck. Jane sat up front again and Tony and me sat in the back. The driver was a young man this time, and the truck wasn't filled with pigs. It had short sideboards.

Tony was silent for a long time; then he said, "I liked it back there."

"You didn't have to leave. You want, we'll stop the driver and walk back with you."

"I just said I liked it there. I didn't say go back. Mrs. Carson was nice."

"Very nice."

"But I wouldn't be with you two if I went back," he said.

"We could come back," I said.

"Sometimes people say they'll do something and they don't," Tony said. "They mean it, but they don't do it."

"I suppose that's true," I said. "But I'll make you a promise. I won't never leave you unless you want to be left. Understand?"

"Yeah," Tony said. "Yeah. I do."

"Good."

Tony didn't say any more about it, and I watched through the rear window as Jane did her magic with the driver. I wondered what lie she was telling this time.

We rode with him almost to the Red River. Then we walked across a bridge, which in that spot wasn't over much of a river at all. After we had been walking on the other side of the bridge for a while, it started to grow dark. There didn't seem to be any good place to stop along the road, so we went off it, to where some trees grew along the river.

As we walked, I got out the flashlight and shone it on the ground in case of water moccasins, which don't like being surprised and are fairly ill-tempered. We hadn't gone far when we saw a campfire in the woods and we could hear people singing.

"What do you think?" Jane said.

"Hobo camp," I said. "It could be a place to rest and maybe share some food, and it could be a place to get our heads stove in."

"They sound cheerful," Jane said.

"Maybe they sing cheerful songs in hell," I said. "You can't tell by that."

Hoboes were all over these days. Thousands of them. Riding the rails and walking along them. Drifting in and out of towns like tumbleweeds blown by the wind. Men, and sometimes women and children. All of them without work, without homes, and without hope. Shuffling about, mostly in worn-out clothes and toeless shoes. Bumming meals from homes along the way, picking through trash and hunting rabbits, sometimes cats and dogs, with nothing more than a heavy stick. Looking for anything to eat. All they had to look forward to was whatever was around the next bend in the road. Mama fed a few from our back door before things got so bad we couldn't feed ourselves. For a while there, they came in droves. When they knew Oklahoma was completely played out, and the people they was begging from was near as bad off as they was, they moved on.

I had always felt sorry for them. Right now, we was just like them. Homeless. No family. And hungry.

"I think we should check it out," Jane said.

"And I'll say what I said again. You don't know who's out there, or what kind of people they are."

It was no use. Jane had already started toward the fire.

We went through a little group of trees and there was a clearing. In the clearing was a fire, and on the fire was a pot, and around the fire was a bunch of hoboes. That made me think there was probably a train track nearby where they could jump on and off.

As we walked up, the singing stopped. Standing close to the fire was a big man with a worn-out jacket and baggy pants and shoes with soles that weren't fully attached. It wasn't really a cold night, but there was something that drew us to them. I suppose that fire seemed cheerful, and we needed all the cheer we could get.

There were four others there. A woman in pants, like Jane—who had gotten a fresh pair from Mrs. Carson—and she had on a big baggy shirt. She was missing some teeth and her hair was cut short. Two of the others looked enough like each other to be brothers, and might have been. There was one other. He was dressed in a suit with a very nice fedora and brand-new two-tone shoes. He was full-faced but kind of handsome in a hangdog manner. I reckon he was thirty or so.

"Hello the fire," I said. I knew from hearing Daddy talk that this was the way you greeted a camp. You let them know you was out there, so as someone with a gun wouldn't part your hair with a bullet or bend a log over your noggin.

"Hello yourself," said the big man. "Come on in."

There were logs and broken-down trees around the fire,

and the folks there were either standing around or sitting on those. We sat down on one of the broken-down trees.

"Can you contribute?" said the big man.

"Beg pardon?" I said.

"Something to add to the pot," he said. "It's right skinny. We got some potatoes boiling in the water, some salt and pepper, and there's even most of an apple in there."

"We do have some things," I said. "How about a can or two of beans, and one of canned hash?"

"Excellent," said the big man. "I'm Jimbo, and the lady here we call Boxcar Bertha, and them two boys that look so much alike are brothers. I don't remember their names."

One of them said, "I'm Sam, he's Joe."

The big man turned to the well-dressed man, said, "This here fella, he brought us the potatoes. What's your name, sir?"

"Floyd," he said.

"He just come up."

"Mighty nice suit you got on, mister," Jane said.

"Thanks," he said. "Maybe not the place for it, but it's what I had on when I had to leave abruptly."

"Leave where?" Jane said.

"A town. By train. I caught it and rode it and got off up the way. I'll catch it out tomorrow."

"Where's it go?" I asked.

"Fort Worth, Texas. I'll get off there because I have to see someone lives there."

"You look to me to be a man that has another line of work besides catching trains," Jane said.

"You might say that," he said, but he didn't offer what

line of work it was. Everyone had gone quiet when Jane had spoken, so I figured it was a rule of the road not to pry unless someone offered you information. I couldn't say that for a fact, not being an experienced hobo and all, but it struck me that way.

"If you kids will take a few dollars and go into town, there's a honky-tonk I passed," said Floyd. "I think they make sandwiches and such. If you go there and knock at the back, I bet they'll let you buy some sandwiches, even if you're too young to go through the front door."

"Actually, I look young for my age," Jane said. "But I'm twenty-one."

I thought: Here we go again.

"You are, are you?" Floyd said. "Well, ma'am, I won't argue with you about it, but they might. I was you, I'd go to the back door. Here's a bill. Take it and get enough sand-wiches for everyone. Get some fat ones with lots of meat, even if you got to pay extra."

Jane went over and took the bill. I saw her hesitate as she pulled it from his fingers. She said, "Would you like one of us to stay here?"

"No," said Floyd. "I trust you. Just hurry. It's about a fifteen-minute walk up there and whatever time it takes to get the food. So half an hour, a little more, you ought to have it, and the stew ought to be boiled out then. We can have stew and sandwiches. You might get some Coca-Colas, and if they'll let you, get a few extra big tin cups for us to dip and eat the stew with. They might have some to sell."

"Okay," Jane said.

Floyd smiled at her. I saw Jane look at him for a long moment. She never looked at me like that.

"All of you can go together if you like," Floyd said. "Just go quick and let's eat."

"All right," she said. "We'll be right back."

I didn't want to leave our goods there, but I didn't want to pick them up and take them with us like we were going to run off or didn't trust the hoboes, which I didn't. But I gave them the cans of food I had promised, and Jimbo had already taken a can opener to them before we had gone outside the glow of the fire and started off through the woods toward the road that led into town.

25

"Do you think we got enough money to buy all that stuff?" I said.

Jane looked at me and smiled. "Boys, take a peek."

She pulled the bill from her pocket and stretched it out between her hands and held it so there was moonlight on it.

It was a hundred-dollar bill.

"Holy cow," Tony said.

"And when he took it out of his pocket, there was a wad of bills. All I saw were hundreds."

"What's a guy with that kind of money and those kind of clothes doing in a hobo camp?" I said.

"Good question," Jane said. "But I'm hungry, and I will not look a gift horse in the mouth."

It was like Floyd had said. About a fifteen-minute walk and we were on the edge of town. I could see the real town nestled in shadows about a hundred yards up the road. There were a few houses and there were lights on in the houses, but there was no one on the street. I figured it was probably about six-thirty or so, but as I said before, I didn't have Daddy's knack for telling time almost to the minute. But the day was done and people had turned into their homes and were getting ready for supper.

Out here on the fringe were the joints. It wasn't exactly the kind of place I wanted to be, but I was hungry and we had a hundred-dollar bill.

At the first joint we come to, we went around to the back. The back door was open and there was hillbilly music coming out of the place, and though there were lights on in there, they were dim. I could hear men talking and women laughing and the clack of pool balls slamming together.

We stood at the back door awhile, but we only saw a few people inside, seated in the center of the place and up near the front.

After a few minutes, Jane said, "Well, hell, I'm going in."

And she went. We went after her.

When we were inside, we were finally noticed. A man with a worn hat that might be white in the daylight, or might once have been white, said, "Well, if they aren't running them a primer school here now."

"Kiss my ass," Jane said.

"Whoa," said the man in the hat to a man swigging from a bottle of beer. "She's got a mouth on her."

The man with the beer said, "Yeah, she does. She talks tough for someone so small."

"I'm tall enough," Jane said.

A woman big enough to go bear hunting with a switch came over and looked at us. She was pale, and her hair was like a bird's nest.

She said, "You kids ain't supposed to be in here."

"Yes, ma'am," I said, trying to jump ahead of Jane starting some kind of wild lie. "We was asked by a man to buy some sandwiches and some cups, if you got them."

"Cups?" she said.

"For dipping stew," Tony said.

"Ah, you're down there in the 'bo camp, ain't you?" she said.

"Yes, ma'am, we are," I said.

"You wanting a handout?" she said. "I can't give no handout. You know how many hoboes come up here looking for a touch? I can't do it. I'd be out of business, broke in a week there's so many."

"We don't want a handout," Jane said. "We said 'buy.' We got money."

She pulled the hundred-dollar bill out of her pocket and took it in both hands and popped it a little like it was a rubber band.

The big woman looked at the bill. "That's money, all right. You ain't supposed to be in here, you know. But where you ought to be and where you are, that's two different things."

She had grown considerably more friendly.

We went over and sat on some stools at the bar. Jane told her what we wanted.

She went in the rear of the place, yelling at a colored man back there about what to make. We could see them through the open double doors. He was at a counter near a stove and he was slicing bread. He didn't like her tone, and he said something back, and then they argued back and forth for a few minutes.

While that was going on, I turned on my stool and saw that the man with the almost-white hat was watching us while he chalked up a pool cue.

"I don't think you should have told him to kiss your ass," I said.

"He'll get over it," Jane said.

The big woman came back to the counter and leaned on it with her elbows, said, "Don't pay no mind to me and Calvin. That's the way we talk."

"Calvin?" Jane said.

"My cook. We always argue. He's been with me ten years. He can cook better than a New York chef, and he works cheaper."

"That's the truth," Calvin said from the kitchen.

"I got to ask," Jane said. "How much the sandwiches going to cost?"

"You want quite a few. Twenty dollars."

"For twelve sandwiches?" Jane said. "What are they made out of? What beef slices cost that much? Are they from the Minotaur?"

"The what?" the big woman said.

"Nothing," Jane said. "Isn't that kind of expensive? Twenty dollars seems like a lot. You can buy sandwiches for a quarter a piece, cheaper sometimes."

"You wanted cups too."

"Still," Jane said.

"These are expensive times," said the big woman.

"These are poor times," Jane said. "Haven't you heard? There's a depression."

"You look like you're doing all right," said the big woman.

"I won't be after I buy these sandwiches."

"I'm throwing in two tin cups," the big woman said.

"You ought to throw in a whole set of dishes and a maid for that price," Jane said. "Heck, you ought to throw in Calvin."

"We don't do that anymore," Calvin called from the back.

"Oh, no offense meant," Jane said.

"That's all right, girl," he said, coming to the counter wiping his hands on a towel. "I knew what you meant. Them sandwiches and cups is all for about eight dollars, and you know it, Magnolia."

The big woman, Magnolia, looked at him like he'd just told someone she was actually a Presbyterian minister on holiday.

"You don't run my business," Magnolia said to Calvin.

109

"Yeah, but I've made enough sandwiches to know what they go for," he said, "and they don't go for that much for that many."

He tossed the towel over his shoulder and went back into the kitchen.

"All right, then," Magnolia said. "Here's the deal, take it or leave it. Twelve fifty."

"That the sandwiches and five tin cups?" Jane asked.

"That's the sandwiches, four tin cups, and my best wishes," Magnolia said.

"That sounds almost fair," Jane said, giving Magnolia the hundred-dollar bill.

26

With our sandwiches and our change from the hundred and our four tin cups, we started back toward the hobo camp. I was carrying the bag of sandwiches, Jane was carrying the bag with Coca-Colas in it. Jane hadn't made the drinks part of the deal, so we paid for those separate, but the price on those had been fair. Everyone knew exactly what a Coca-Cola cost.

Tony had the four cups tied together with a string, and he was carrying those.

We hadn't gone too far when I said, "Those men from the joint. They're following us."

It was the one with the hat and the one that was drinking the beer. They were walking kind of fast, and were right behind us. We crossed the road and headed for where the woods grew up, and they crossed the road with us.

I heard a snick, and when I looked back, the one with the hat had a knife open. The moonlight caught on it, and in that moment, that four-inch blade looked as big to me as a machete.

"We're going to need the rest of that money," said the man with the knife.

The other man said, "Yeah, and we'll take them sandwiches too."

"Really," Jane said, turning, looking at them. "You're so low you'd rob three kids of their money, and even take their sandwiches?"

"You forgot to mention the cups and the Coca-Colas," said the man with the hat.

I stepped in front of Jane. "You go on back where you come from. You might have a knife, but you still got a fight coming."

"I'll cut you from gut to gill," said the man with the knife.

"Oh, you boys don't want to do that," said a voice.

We turned, and there was Floyd coming up from the woods, walking fast.

"This ain't your trouble," said the man with the hat.

"Sure it is," said Floyd. "Couple of those sandwiches are mine."

"Oh, well, we didn't know that," said the other man.

"So, if I hadn't come up, you was going to take them from the kids, but now a grown man comes up, you got another line of talk?"

"I don't know," said the man with the hat and the knife. "Maybe I'm talking too soon. I got the knife."

"Fella," said Floyd, "you'd have been better off to have brought yourself a peppermint stick. They're a whole sight easier to eat."

That took the hat-wearing man by surprise.

While he was thinking it over, Floyd said, "You know, as much as I'd like to knock your heads together, I'm hungry and don't want to take the time." He pushed back his coat and reached around to the small of his back and pulled out a little revolver. "Just put the knife away and go on back to being drunk and stupid. My figuring is that's what you do best."

"Whoa," said the man with the hat. "We ain't looking for that kind of trouble."

"What kind you looking for?" Floyd said. "I can come up with all kinds of trouble. What kind do you need?"

"No kind."

"Yeah," Floyd said, holding the gun down to his side. "You don't want trouble, then I think you ought not to go fishing for it. You might catch something."

The man in the hat folded up the knife and put it in his pocket. "We'll go on back," he said.

"That's a sensible idea," Floyd said. "You kids think that's sensible?"

"I know I do," Jane said.

Tony and I agreed.

The two men didn't say anything else. They just turned and walked back toward the honky-tonk.

"How come you come along?" Jane said, when the men were up the road a piece.

"I didn't want to go up and get the food myself," Floyd said, "which is why I sent you, but I got to thinking. You kids with all that money, and this not exactly being the general store. Figured I might ought to come up and make sure things was all right, since you going was my fault."

"Was it because you actually thought we might run off with your money?" Jane asked.

"Nope," Floyd said. "Easy come, easy go."

"Maybe you was worried just a little bit?" Jane said.

"All right," Floyd said. "Just a little bit."

27

Back in camp, we ate the sandwiches and the stew. We gave our spare cup to Boxcar Bertha, and she gave us all some pieces of peppermint that looked as if they might have been sucked on before and had lint on them.

We ate them anyway.

We sang songs and talked, and Jimbo told ghost stories about headless men, and haints that came out of brick walls when you passed and grabbed you and took you with them inside the wall and mixed up your insides and turned your feet around so that when you was put back, you had to walk backwards.

I don't know I believe in ghosts, but I sure like stories about them. The ones Jimbo told, or maybe it was the way he told them, made the hairs on the back of my neck stand up like hog bristles. That night I dreamed me and Jane and Tony were walking along in the dark next to a long and very tall brick wall. We walked and then we heard something. We turned to look, and it was Bad Tiger and Timmy, stepping right out of the bricks. They grabbed us and pulled us into the wall. I woke up panting, and it took me a good while to get back to sleep. I didn't dream about the wall or Bad Tiger and Timmy anymore, but I sure remembered the dream when I woke up.

Next morning, except for us and Floyd, everyone else stayed in camp. Bertha had a later train to catch, and I don't know what the others had plans to do, or if they had plans at all. They didn't strike me as folks with someplace to be at any certain time.

We packed out of there, and as we walked toward the trainyard, Jane stepped along beside Floyd. She said, "Thanks for helping us last night. That was something."

"It wasn't anything. They brought a knife to a gunfight."

"Would you have used that gun?"

"I'd rather not."

"But would you?"

"If I had to."

"Have you used it before?" she asked.

"You might be a mite too curious. What are you, a cat?"

"I just like to know things," she said. "I'm going to be a reporter."

"Girls do that?"

"I don't know about girls," Jane said, "but women do. And if they don't, I'm going to do it anyway."

"I bet you will," Floyd said.

Pretty soon we could see some cars parked along the street. Across the way, we could see train tracks and the rail-yard. On some of the tracks were a few boxcars, none of them hooked to engines.

All of a sudden, Floyd pulled us up behind one of the cars.

115

"I'm going to take a guess here," he said, "and figure ain't none of you kids caught a train before."

"That's a good guess," I said.

"Well now," Floyd said. "First thing you got to watch for is the bulls."

"Bulls?" Jane said. "You mean like cattle?"

"No. I mean the train bulls. They're like cops for the trainyard. They can be mighty mean. They don't want you on those trains, and they might just snap a nightstick upside your head. I know a fella got hit and didn't never get over it. He sometimes thinks I'm his grandma."

"Really?" Tony asked.

"Yeah," Floyd said, "when he don't think I'm a little red hen. It was quite a lick. What you got to do is get up there close, not get seen, and not be up there too soon. You get close when the train slows down. It don't stop here, it just slows down, and that's perfect for a ride."

"If the train bulls don't get you," I said.

"Yeah," Floyd said, "and if you don't fall between the cars and get run over and lose a leg or an arm or get mashed altogether. And if someone isn't already in the boxcar that's got a bad attitude."

"We can ride with you, can't we?" Jane asked.

"If we manage to get on the same car," Floyd said. "But that might not happen. You get what you get in this kind of business."

"I still say you're well dressed for a train jumper," Jane said.

We heard the train coming from a distance. It blew its whistle.

Jane moved forward. Floyd caught her by the shoulder. "Not yet. Too soon, a bull might see you."

"I don't see any bulls," Jane said.

"That don't mean they ain't there," Floyd said.

"Then why catch the train here?" Jane asked.

"Because this is where it slows down to make the curve. Out there," Floyd said, waving a hand toward where the tracks disappeared into some woods, "it's running top speed, or a good speed, anyway. This is the spot. Now, I'm going to point you to the train that goes to Fort Worth, but after that, it's every man for himself. And woman. I didn't take you kids in to raise."

"We're perfectly fine at raising ourselves," Jane said. Then she added: "Of course, any tips that might get us on the train without being killed are very much appreciated."

Floyd grinned.

"All right, tell you what. I'm going to get you on that train. I'll do that much."

"Thanks, mister," Tony said.

"Don't thank me now," Floyd said. "You ain't on the train yet."

Soon as I saw the train my stomach started to flutter. Thinking about jumping on a train is one thing, but actually doing it while it's moving, slowing down or not, is another thing altogether.

We started running. Down near the station, coming out from behind a parked boxcar, we saw a man dressed in black. He had on a black cap, and he had a nightstick in his hand. I don't know if it was a uniform or if he just liked to dress that way.

117

He saw us and yelled something.

Floyd hollered out, "Run like hell!"

We took off running for the train. It was slowing, but I didn't think it was slowing enough. The sacks we were carrying were heavy and weighed us down.

I looked back, and the man with the nightstick was gaining on us. As we got near the train, Floyd yelled, "Grab on and climb in!"

Easier said than done, but it did seem as if the train was slowing even more. We picked out an open boxcar and went for it. Jane slung her sack in the open door, and she jumped first. She was nimble as a deer. She hit the floor of the open boxcar with her palms and she was up and in. I had to keep running. Finally I was close enough to throw my bag inside and grab and swing myself up. Jane got hold of me and helped pull me in.

When we looked back, Floyd had Tony on his shoulders and was running alongside the car as if Tony weighed no more than his hat.

Floyd flung his hat into the open boxcar, snatched Tony off his shoulders while he was running, and sort of stuck him at the car. Me and Jane grabbed him and pulled him on board. Tony had lost his sack of goods.

We could hear Floyd breathing loudly as he ran. In the next moment, he was grabbing at it and climbing on board and we were helping him.

The bull hadn't given up. He was winded too, and he sounded like a busted accordion when he ran, but he was closing in.

Floyd was almost inside when the bull hit his leg with the nightstick. Floyd let out a groan and turned so that he was facing out of the car. As the bull came closer again, huffing and puffing and having lost his hat, Floyd kicked out and caught him in the face and the bull tumbled backwards and did a flip.

"Eat them apples!" Floyd yelled.

The train began to pick up speed. It had been slowing all the while this was going on, but now it was starting to go faster and faster, and there wasn't any way that bull could catch up, even if he'd been on a bicycle, or a horse. We was hauling now; the wind blowing by like we was in a little tornado.

We looked back and the bull was getting up and yelling at us and shaking his nightstick.

"That don't get nothing done," Floyd yelled at him. "We're already gone."

The bull turned into a little dot.

Tony said, "Look there."

We turned to look at the back end of the boxcar. An old man was lying inside with his back up against the corner. He was looking at us, but he didn't look as if he thought we were really there. He looked completely tuckered out. His cheeks was dirty and had fell into themselves like sinkholes. His hair was thin, and the pieces of it that was left looked like they had been drawn on his head with a pencil.

I went over to him and the others followed. I said, "Are you okay?"

He opened his watery eyes and looked up at me. "I'm just

about gone. That's what I am." When he spoke, his tongue came out of his mouth, it was so thick and dry. When it did it touched the few bottom teeth he had left and wiggled them around like loose fence posts in a high wind.

Floyd was there now. He bent down and said, "What's wrong with you, pops?"

"I done got old. Worn out."

"What you look like to me is hungry," Floyd said. "When did you eat last?"

"I don't know," the old man said. "I can't remember."

"If you can't remember when you ate last," Floyd said, "then that's too long. Jack, you mind giving him something from your sack?"

I nodded and started digging in it. I came up with my can opener and a couple of cans. One was soup and the other was meat. I opened them and gave them to him with a spoon.

The old man started to eat.

Floyd grabbed his hand, said, "You eat, but you got to slow it down, or you'll just puke it all up. Take a bite, chew a long time. Drink the soup slow."

"I ain't got nothing much left to chew with," the old man said.

Jane had come up with a couple more cans, but Floyd shook his head and she put them back in her bag.

The man ate slowly like he was told. He closed his eyes sometimes while he chewed. He ate like it was the first time he had ever tasted food. I was glad I had given him soup, and that the meat was some kind of ham that was easy to chew.

We just stayed where we were and listened to the train

chug and clank along and watched the old man eat. He ate the meat and drank the soup like it was water.

After a while, he paused and looked up at us.

"I feel a little better," he said.

"See there," Floyd said. "You ain't done for. You're just hungry."

The old man smiled at us. "Oh, I'm done, all right. But at least I won't go away hungry."

"You'll be all right," Floyd said. "You just take it easy. Here, stretch out."

Floyd got the old man under the shoulders and helped him stretch out. Then Floyd crushed his nice hat up and put it under the old man's head and covered him with his suit coat.

The old man went straight to sleep.

"I miss my old man," Floyd said. "He reminds me some of him."

"That was an awfully nice thing to do," Jane said.

"It wasn't nothing," Floyd said. "It ain't nothing at all. Something like that," he said, straightening his coat over the old man so that it covered him better, "is like the little boy who stuck his finger in a hole in the dike. It don't really work, and it don't hold back nothing for long. It's just another moment he's got."

"Well," Jane said. "It's another moment, then."

"Yeah," Floyd said. "It's that, all right. But it ain't nothing else."

28

"Thing to do when you get to Fort Worth," Floyd said, "is get off. This train is going to slow, but it ain't going to stop. I've ridden it before. You got to jump off before you get into the station, and then you got to walk up close to the station and get another train that goes to Tyler, and then you got to get off there, 'cause its next stop is Lindale, which is a little burg outside of Tyler. You understand?"

We said that we did.

"I can't help you after we get off," he said. "I got business to take care of. I can't be messing with you kids."

"You've treated us fine," I said.

"You have," Jane said, and the way she looked at him made me a little jealous.

"I'm glad I could help," he said. "But after Fort Worth you're on your own."

"We understand," I said.

"I'd rather you stay with us," Jane said.

"Can't," Floyd said.

Floyd looked back at the old man.

"What about him?" I said.

"Time's got him by the leg," Floyd said, "and it's holding on tight, and it's tugging him away, and I'm pretty sure it ain't going to give him back."

After a while we pulled some cans of food out of our bags and shared them with Floyd, and then we all found a place to sit down with our backs against the car, and with the train rocking on the tracks and the excitement we'd had, we all drifted off to sleep.

We rode like that a long ways, and when we did wake up, none of us had much to say. We went back to sleep. That was how it worked until the train rolled us in a few miles outside of the Fort Worth trainyards. We could see them in the distance.

Floyd said, "All right, now. Coming up is the jump-off spot. We all jump off there. I point you to your train, and then I'm gone."

The old man was awake now, and he had sat up with his back against the boxcar. He straightened out Floyd's hat and his coat and laid them over his knees.

"You're going to be needing these, son," the old man said.

"Yes, sir," Floyd said. "I suppose I will."

As Floyd went over and got his hat and coat, the old man looked up, said, "You're him, ain't you?"

"Him who?"

"Pretty Boy Floyd."

"I don't like being called that."

"But you're him just the same, ain't you?"

123

"Charles is my first name," Floyd said. "I don't like none of that Pretty Boy business."

"I don't care what they say," the old man said. "You ain't bad in my book. You could run over a child on a tricycle and shoot the eye out of a one-legged librarian lady, and I'd still be on your side."

Floyd laughed. "You don't have to worry about me doing nothing like that. And don't believe everything you read in the papers. I done all that stuff they say I did, robbed all them banks they claim I'd robbed, there'd have to be four of me, and a couple more to rest up for later."

Floyd put his coat and hat on, said, "You need some help getting out of the boxcar, pops?"

"I ain't never getting off," the old man said. "This is my home. I stay here, and I die here. Ain't no one going to miss me."

"Someone will," said Floyd.

"No," the old man said. "They won't."

"I'll think about you, then," Floyd said.

"Do that, boy. Do that for me."

"I will," Floyd said, tipping his hat. "But I don't want my last thought of you to be that I left you on a train and you couldn't get off. I bet we could help you off. These folks are riding to Tyler. You could ride with them."

"I'll give it a shot," the old man said, "but I don't know how much I got left in me."

"Why don't we find out? What's your name, pops?"

"Daggart."

"All right, then, Daggart. You ready?"

"No," said Daggart, "but the way I see it, if I can't jump out of this train, I can darn sure fall out of it."

"That's the spirit," Floyd said.

29

I got an arm around one side of Daggart, and Floyd got the other side. Me and him jumped with the old man, hit the ground, and tumbled some. It was grassy there and kind of wooded, so we had a soft landing and were partly hid behind the trees. The old man took the fall well enough. We helped him up and he seemed okay. Worst I got was a mouthful of dirt and grass. After all the sand I'd seen, that bit of grass was pretty nice. Back in Oklahoma, green was as rare as a solid meal.

Behind us, Jane and Tony jumped and landed safely. When it was all said and done, we managed to get off without breaking a leg or twisting an ankle.

"Now," Floyd said. "You see the tracks on the other side of the trees? I've caught that line before. It goes to Tyler. It don't stop once it gets rolling, so that's the one you want. It'll take you all the way in. There's enough of a slant on the other side of them trees, you get to moving downhill pretty quick, you can make the boxcar easy. It's kind of like a porch that leads down to it. It's high up and slanted about right, though you got to get off to a good run."

"I can't run," Daggart said. "Maybe I can just roll down and onto it."

"You'd roll down and under it," Jane said.

"Hell, I know that," Daggart said. "I was kidding. Didn't you know I was kidding?"

"Good," Jane said. "You're up to joking. That's an improvement."

"All I'm saying," Daggart said, "is I've caught it here before. I just don't know I can do it today. I don't know I want to go to Tyler."

"You're just being contrary," Jane said.

"A little, I reckon," he said. "Maybe it's because I feel like death warmed over with a match, and the heat's fading."

"We'll stay with you," I said. "At least until we can get you settled somewhere."

"Ain't no place to settle me," he said.

"We'll do what we can," I said.

He sat down with his back against a little pine and looked down the tracks. A few seconds later, he said, "Guess going with you folks is a mite better than just sitting here in these trees and dying."

"You got to think more positive," Jane said. "You got to see what's down the road a bit."

"I done seen what's down there. There's just more road."

In the cover of the trees, we squatted and waited, the old man still sitting with his back against the pine.

Up a ways ahead of us, I saw there was at least a half-dozen hoboes in the trees and brush, waiting on that train. They looked back at us in a manner that made me a little nervous. We wouldn't be the only ones riding, and there might be some trouble if we weren't careful.

"Try and get the same boxcar, if you can," Floyd said. "That way you can watch out for one another if there's some-one else in the car that might take a mind to bother you. But let me tell you, they got a gun, a knife, it's best to give them what they want or jump."

"That won't be much," Jane said. "Our bag of goods and a few dollars is all we got."

"It ain't worth dying over," Floyd said.

"You didn't give them sandwiches away the other night," Tony said.

"No," Floyd said. "But I was meaner than them, and I had a gun. I ain't proud of that gun. It ain't brought me much good, except that time the other night. A gun just seems to make things go bad. You start to depend on it and give it too much respect. I wish I hadn't never seen one."

"Is that the train?" Daggart said.

We looked down the track. A train was moving out of the station.

"That's the one heading southeast," Floyd said. "The one you want."

"Could the line have changed since you rode it last?" Jane said.

"Sure it could have," Floyd said. "But you don't want to

think about that, do you? But you miss it, there's tomorrow, about this same time. It leaves out when the Fort Worth train comes in. I know that much from having been here and known people who've ridden it."

"I guess it's in for a penny, in for a pound," Jane said. "Bend down."

Floyd studied her for a moment; then he bent closer to her face and she kissed him on the cheek.

"Thanks for being so kind," she said.

"Pass it along," Floyd said. "I ain't passed near enough of it along before, so you do it for me. Say you will."

"We'll do that," I said.

Floyd shook my and Tony's hands. He bent down and shook Daggart's hand. The old man was still resting against that pine tree. Floyd touched his shoulder.

"Goodbye and good luck," Floyd said, and with that he moved across the track well in front of the oncoming train, turned, and waved at us, and then the train's engine passed in front of him, followed by the train, and then we couldn't see him anymore.

30

As the train began to move closer, we watched for an open boxcar. A number of closed ones passed. Finally we saw an open one, but those hoboes charged down from the trees and dove right into it.

I could see there was a line of open boxcars behind that one. I turned and got hold of Daggart's arm to help him up, but he was deadweight.

I bent down and looked at him. "He's gone, Jane," I said.

In just those few moments, he'd given it up. What was left of Daggart had flown out of him and gone the way of last year. His eyes were still open, and so was his mouth. A fly had already landed on his bottom lip. I waved it away.

"Least he didn't suffer none," Jane said. "And he was with folks he liked."

"He didn't even know us," I said.

"I figure he knew us enough. His last memories are of people being nice to him."

"There ain't no sense to nothing," Tony said. "I don't want to ride no train."

"Yes you do," Jane said, grabbing him and pushing him in the direction of the tracks.

"We ought to do something," I said. "We ought not just leave him."

"We can't wait," Jane said. "He's gone and there isn't a thing we can do. And that train's going to be gone too. I don't want to hide somewhere and wait until tomorrow. He's dead and that's it. We done what we could."

I closed Daggart's eyes with my fingers. It wasn't a perfect job, but his lids mostly covered them over.

"Come on," Jane said, and grabbed my arm. "You got to come on now."

Then she let go of me, and she and Tony were darting down the hill toward the train.

I looked one more time at Daggart. "Sorry," I said. "Burying folks don't seem to be our stong suit."

I ran down the hill after them then. I could see they had already reached a boxcar and were struggling on board. The train was starting to move fast. I ran as hard as I could.

"Come on, Jack!" Jane shouted. "Now ain't the time to get lazy."

I ran so hard I thought my heart would burst. I finally got up alongside the open boxcar and got hold of it, but my hand slipped and I nearly stumbled onto the rails and beneath the train.

For a moment there, I thought about quitting. I thought about letting the train go and just going back up into the trees and leaning up against a pine next to poor old Daggart. But then I thought about my daddy, how he had quit when

130

things got bad, and decided I wasn't going to be a quitter in any kind of way. I ran even harder. The sweat flew off me as I ran. Or at least I thought it was sweat at first. Then I realized that some of it was, but not all. Some of it was tears.

A moment later and the train would have picked up too much speed for me to make it, but I got a ladder down from the open boxcar and pulled myself up on that and rested a minute. Jane stuck her head out of the car and grinned at me.

I grinned back.

After a few minutes, I climbed up on the hitch, found the ladder that led to the top of the boxcar, and went up there. Then I swung down from the top and stuck my legs inside. Tony and Jane grabbed me and helped pull me in.

We sat up against the side of the car. There wasn't anyone in it but us.

Jane said, "How about that? We met Pretty Boy Floyd and he befriended us."

"Who's Pretty Boy Floyd?" Tony said.

"He's famous," Jane said.

"A criminal," I said. "That's who he is."

"He was all right," Jane said.

"He robs banks and steals stuff from people," I said, and I knew I was telling the truth, and I stand by it to this day, but I knew too some of it was my jealousy talking. Still, I couldn't help myself. I hadn't liked the way Jane had kissed him on the cheek.

"He didn't steal nothing from us," Tony said.

"No," Jane said, "he didn't."

"He's still a criminal," I said.

"I liked him," Tony said. "He was good to that old man, and he ran with me on his shoulders."

"He robs banks," I said.

"Banks haven't treated people so good," Jane said. "You can rob someone with a gun, or you can do it with a fountain pen. A mark here and there and they can foreclose on your property."

"They was talking about doing it to us," Tony said. "Taking our farm."

"By now, they have," Jane said. "With Pa dead, ain't no one to pay for it. Hell, they can have it. It wasn't nothing but a sandpit anyhow."

"I reckon ours is gone too," I said, "but Floyd is still a criminal."

"Yeah, he is," Jane said, "but he isn't like Bad Tiger or Timmy. They started out sideways. Pretty Boy just got turned that way and couldn't get back."

"You can't know that," I said.

"I think I'm a pretty good guesser."

I crossed my arms and looked at the floor.

"You jealous of him?" Jane said.

"No."

"I think you are," she said.

"Maybe a little. He ain't one of your knights, Jane. He ain't Sir Galahad."

"He's about as close as I'm going to get to a knight. Let me believe that, even if it is only for a moment."

"That's silly," I said.

"Listen here, Jack. A kiss on the cheek isn't the same as a kiss on the lips. I don't want you to make too much out of that. Both kinds of kisses are friendly, but the lips is more friendly. It means more."

I studied her face. It was hard to know when that girl was lying.

"Really?" I said.

"Really," she said, and winked at me.

31

It's the solid truth that when we were riding that train to Tyler, it was the lowest I'd ever been. Even lower than when my folks died. Reason was, them dying was just then coming home to roost. It wasn't like I didn't know they were dead, but when I saw that old man, all of a sudden I realized it was real. It had taken me a while, and I guess I had sort of been stunned all that time, but right then I could feel it come down on me heavy as a falling house.

I just sat there with my back against the boxcar so I had a

view out the open door and thought about Mama dying, and then Daddy doing what he did, and me burying them in the barn. Then I thought about Jane and Tony coming along, and us going over and stealing a dead man's car. Next, there had been Buddy, shot by his own partners, and now Daggart, dying while waiting to catch a train. All I could think of was his eyes staring at nothing, and just before that he had been talking and seeing what we were seeing. It was sobering to realize life came and then it went.

It was hard to see how things would get any better. Right then I was feeling that boxcar bouncing over the tracks and it was shaking me down to my bones. I guess the wind was tearing me up, even if I wasn't right in the doorway, 'cause my eyes got so full of tears I had to use the back of my sleeve to wipe them dry. And I must have been hungry, 'cause my belly started seizing up and cramping.

I glanced at Jane, who had put her back against the boxcar and had her eyes closed. She looked pretty sweet when she was asleep. I decided then and there that Jane was about as big a blowhard as there was, but at the bottom of her bucket there was something real. She knew life was short, and she lived like it was and sucked all the juice out of it. I told myself right then and there I was going to do the same, even if I knew I'd never be quite like Jane. Wasn't nobody could get to the juice the way she could, and wasn't nobody ever who could enjoy it as much as she did, even the times when it was sour.

Looking at Tony, I could see he was weakening, and it wasn't just from the trip and eating kind of here and there, never getting any solid rest, and seeing what he had seen. It was like there was a hole in the top of his head and you could almost see him easing out of it.

He turned and looked at me and tried to smile. The corner of one side of his mouth lifted up and fell down, like a window blind that hadn't caught good when you pulled the cord to raise it.

There were tears in his eyes.

I glanced back at Jane.

She opened her eyes while I was looking, smiled at me, got up, and come over to the edge of the boxcar. She sat down in the wide doorway and let her feet dangle over the edge. The sun was on her face, and it lit her up good. The way she looked, you would have thought she'd been given the keys to everything there was in life that was good. She was grinning a little. She was in her element. She was born for adventure. And she couldn't have been happier.

I guess she thought about the same things I had been thinking about, the loss of her family and all, but she could move on quick. Daggart was maybe not forgotten, but she sure wasn't sweating over him. He was dead and gone and we weren't. That was how she saw things. It was now, and it was all about the living.

"That's some pretty country," she said.

I wanted to answer, but I was afraid my voice would crack. The wind was making my eyes water again. I turned so I wasn't looking right at her.

The train clattered along and slowed here and there, and

we even had a guy jump in our car as we got into East Texas and it slowed going through a station. He wasn't as ragged as some. He had dark hair and a face that wasn't as lined as those of most men on the road. He had on good shoes, which made me think he had been someone important once. The leather on them squeaked as he walked to the back of the boxcar. He spoke to us kindly and sat down with his knees pulled up under his chin. If he had any curiosity about us, he kept it to himself.

I put my hand in my pocket and pulled out my pocketknife so he couldn't see it, kept it down by my leg so that I could pop it open. It was that kind of knife. A flick of the wrist and you had raw blade.

But he didn't bother us. He rode to the next town, said goodbye, and got off.

I put the knife away.

I moved to where I could let my legs hang like Jane was doing. Tony came and sat down between us.

We passed lots of green and lots of water. At first glance, after where we had been, you could mistake it for paradise. But after a while we saw shacks and old cars and people walking, wearing clothes that had been patched so much they wasn't nothing but patches.

We passed little farms where chickens ran loose and so did the kids.

We passed sawmills, and we could see the tall sheds that housed the great blades of the mill, and we could hear the blades whining through the lumber, throwing up sawdust like sand in a windstorm. There were glimpses of long trucks and ox-drawn wagons and some with teams of mules, hauling the lumber out.

Finally we passed a river. Jane said it was the Sabine. I reckoned that was so, but I didn't know for sure, and there wasn't no use asking her if she was sure. She'd just lie about it. There were some people sitting on a long wooden bridge over the river with lines in the water. Farther down, we saw some kids on the bank fishing. Two boys and a little girl. They waved at us as we went by, and we waved back.

The sky was clear for a long time, and then all of a sudden the air got cool and clouds dark as the bottom of a well rolled in. With them came flashes of lightning and rolls of thunder. The rain hammered the earth and the wind whipped the trees, making the tops of them slash at the sky. We had to pull completely back inside the car to keep from getting wet. It had been a long time since we'd seen a real rain. One with all the power of the heavens behind it, wetting up the earth and making the air smell like dirt. For me, it was like something religious was happening. Like a thing denied me for a long time was now being given, and there was a lot of it.

The trees on the side of the track were close, and they were dark with shadow, but from time to time the lightning came and for a moment the inside of the boxcar was bright as day.

Along the tree-shadowed tracks we went, into the dark rain, and finally into the dark night that was cut open here and there by bright swords of lightning. The air shook the train with explosions of thunder.

Finally we lay in the center of the car and closed our eyes.

We didn't talk at all. I just lay there thinking on things, and none of the things I was thinking on were cheering me up much, except maybe that rain. The air felt so cool, and it was dark with cloud shadow. But the rain was all there was that was good right then. I just couldn't get away from all that had happened back home, from Mama and Daddy down in the dry earth. I hoped it was raining there.

I tried to feel better by thinking about finding Strangler and about us warning him that Bad Tiger and Timmy were coming. But I kept thinking it wasn't going to be easy, and Bad Tiger and Timmy were looking too. They might have already found him. We might never find him. And no matter what Strangler was wanting to do with the money, he was still the same as them. Same as Pretty Boy Floyd. They were all crooks. Maybe some crooks are better people than other crooks, but they're all crooks.

I thought about Jane's East Texas relatives. She didn't even know their names. I assumed they had the same last name as her, but then I come to realize that she hadn't actually told me if her original kin was the uncle or the aunt. If it was the aunt, then she'd most likely taken up her husband's name. And on top of that, wasn't anything that said they'd be glad to see her and Tony, let alone me, who wasn't no kin at all.

What it came down to was we were just sort of out there in the wind.

Still, trying to stop someone from being killed had to be the right thing to do. It would be nice to save someone once. Or if they died, to bury someone once, or see to it that they were buried. We were sort of like bad luck charms. Wherever we went, a dead body was bound to show up before long, and it was bound to be left unburied or unreported. It was a knack.

In time, the lightning and the thunder were less frequent, and there was just the wind and the rain. The rain was cold enough that we huddled together and pulled our two bags close to us until we were a little warm from each other's bodies. The rocking of the train and the rattle and the squeaking of the wheels on the track became comforting.

Even damp and cold and unhappy, I slept.

32

Come early morning the rain was long gone. The sun was warm, and the trees, mostly tall pines, had become thicker along the track. There was water that could be seen between the pines, and those spots of water were shiny like the wet scales of a fish. But mostly there were shadows from the trees, and they lay across the water like dark logs. They were so dark it made the bright spots seem even brighter.

We got some food from our bags and sat in the doorway

eating it. The day began to brighten and the shadows from the trees on the water shifted and faded and pretty soon the water was clear and bright except where there was moss and plants on the surface or growing up out of it. Birds were fluttering from tree to tree. All kinds of birds. Bluebirds and redbirds and mockingbirds and sparrows. Before long it turned hot.

I watched the water go by. There wasn't a river or a creek, but there were some big pools out there. I thought I might like to get some worms and a pole and fish it. I knew some of the water was fed by a creek somewhere. There would be fish in the deep parts. Not big fish, but hungry fish that I could catch and eat. I was hungry all the time. Some place inside of me was always empty.

We passed a crossing where a pickup waited on the train. The pickup was stuffed with kids. When they saw us they waved at us, but we went by so quick we didn't have time to wave back.

"I saw a sign," Jane said. "It said Tyler, four miles."

"We'll be there pretty quick," I said.

"Yeah," Jane said, "and my thinking is we'll start slowing down soon. I think when it's slow enough we ought to jump off right away and not even mess with being close to the station and those bulls."

"It may not slow enough," Tony said.

"It will," she said. The way she talked, you'd have thought she'd been a hobo for twenty years.

But she was right. Not long after, the train began to slow. And then it slowed a lot. I leaned out the door and looked up the track. There was nothing to see.

"I think it's better to walk a little," Jane said, "than be in sight of the station."

"You said that," I said.

"Yeah," she said, "but I wasn't sure anyone was listening."

We got our bags, and when we came to a place where there was some thick-looking grass, we tossed our bags and jumped.

I couldn't stop tumbling on the grass, and finally I fetched up against a tree with my feet in the air and my back on the ground. By the time I was on my feet, Jane had both our bags and Tony was scrambling. She brought me mine and I threw it over my shoulder. The three of us started walking along the edge of the track. The train was still going by, but it didn't take long before it left us. We could hear those boxcars rattling for a long time, and we could see the smoke from the engine hanging in the air and we could smell it.

After a long time walking, I said, "Are you sure it said four miles and not forty miles?"

"I been thinking about that," Jane said. "Actually, I just saw a four. But there might have been a number in front of it. Or behind it. But I did see a four."

I stopped. "That's a big difference from saying it was four miles, and now you're saying you don't know if it was four or fourteen or almost any number that either begins or ends with four."

"I guess I got a little excited," Jane said. "I wanted to get off. And the train did slow, didn't it?"

I was starting to think it had just slowed because of a bad curve, and not because we were near a station, but I didn't feel any need to say it right then. It didn't matter. We were off the train.

"I'm tired of walking," Tony said. "And it's hot."

"There's plenty of trees," Jane said. "We can find shade."

"And with all those pools of water," I said, "we can find mosquitoes in the shade."

"And dad-burned snakes," Tony said. "I don't like snakes."

"You both are such pessimists," Jane said. "Where is your spirit of adventure?"

"Who says I have to have one?" I said.

33

It was like I figured. Jane had read the sign wrong because she hadn't paid attention or because, like she said, she wanted off the train. Whatever, it was more than any four miles, and it was starting to get dark by the time we did see a sign for a town.

But it wasn't Tyler. It was Winona, and the sign said WEL-COME TO WINONA, POPULATION 340. Fact was, it was pretty much just a hole in the road with a couple of stores. Stopping at one of the stores, we decided to buy some Coca-Colas and eat some of our food. We opened up our sacks and got our can openers and had some beans, which I was getting really tired of. They wasn't doing my stomach any good either, and on more than a few occasions as of late, I'd had to make a point of walking behind Jane and Tony so if I passed wind it wouldn't make things difficult for my traveling companions. And I darn sure didn't want that sort of thing to happen when I was next to Jane. I couldn't hardly even live with the idea of it.

Tony, however, was less concerned. He was more than willing to run up in front of us and let it fly and laugh about it.

But now we were in town and we sat on a bench under an oak by the side of the road and ate our beans and drank our Coca-Colas and watched it get dark. Fireflies were starting to move under the tree, and I could see them across the streets and in the yards where there were houses. Unlike at home, these houses weren't piled with sand, their paint stripped off by it blowing and gritting the color away. They were painted, and the grass in the yards was green, and the trees were tall and full of leaves. Squirrels were in the trees. I watched them play. A man in the house across the way came out on the porch and cleared his throat in a way that made me feel a little sick, and then spat a stream of whatever had been down in his chest out into the yard. It was so loud it startled the squirrels. The man went back inside.

A man in a new car pulled up at the curb and got out. He was a short man with a big straw hat, and his belly fell over his belt like it was trying to find some comfortable place to lie down.

He came over to where we sat and put his boot on the

edge of the bench, right by me, and wiped the top of it off with a red kerchief he took out of his pants pocket. "You kids live here?"

"No," I said.

"I didn't figure you did," he said. "Haven't seen you around here before."

"We're just passing through," Jane said. "Truth is, we inherited a little oil money over in Tyler, so we're trying to get there, and we got our train tickets mixed up and ended up off the train."

"Tickets, huh?" the man said, and snapped the handkerchief loudly, then folded it and put it back in his pants pocket.

"That's right," Jane said.

"From the looks of you," he said, "and looking at your luggage," he said, eyeing our bags, "my guess is your ticket was how fast you could run and jump inside a boxcar."

"We rode a boxcar," Jane said. "That part is right. But that's because there was that ticket mix-up. Where was it, Jack? Fort Worth?"

I didn't know what to do, so I just nodded.

"So we didn't have tickets, even though they were paid for, and when we borrowed a phone and called our relatives in Tyler, they were out. We decided to just go on and catch a train hobo-style and ride in."

"This ain't Tyler," the man said.

"No," Jane said. "I was just explaining to my cousin Jack here, that he had us jump off the train too soon. Right, Jack?"

"Sure," I said.

"If this is your cousin," the man said, "who's the little one?"

"I ain't that little," Tony said. "I'm young."

"That's my brother, Tony," Jane said.

"Uh-huh," said the man. "Well now, I got an idea for you. You can take it or leave it, but I figure on your way to your rich inheritance, you might be in need of money, 'cause Tyler, that's still a good twelve, fifteen miles away as the crow flies. And since you ain't no crows, maybe for you three it's twenty-five walking by the highway, if you don't get a ride. You might want to take yourself a break for a while if you need some pocket money, and a job might be something you'd consider."

"We don't need a job," Jane said.

As much as I didn't like eating beans, I had noted that when we opened our bags, we were down to one can of beans per bag. There were two bags and three of us. We did have some cooking gear, flashlights, and the like, but you couldn't eat that.

I said, "What kind of job?"

"Fieldwork," he said.

I had done plenty of that, and so had Jane and Tony. It was our background.

"I don't want any fieldwork," Jane said.

"You've done it before," I said.

"Which is why I don't want any more of it."

"There's better things than picking peas," said the man, "but that's what I got, and I'm offering a dollar a day for each of you for an honest day's work."

"Tony ain't nothing but a kid," I said.

"Kids working all over this country," he said. "What makes him any different?"

"That's hard work for a kid for a dollar a day," I said.

"That's hard work for anyone for a dollar a day," Jane said.

The man took his boot off the bench and straightened his hat like he needed to adjust it for the wind, but there wasn't any.

"Considering you've done this kind of work before," the man said, "if I can take your word for it—"

"You can," I said.

"Then I'll give you each a dollar fifty a day."

"That's not any better," Jane said.

"There's plenty that would take the dollar," he said.

"Yeah," Jane said. "Where are they?"

"They'll show up."

"Then let them," Jane said.

The man pursed his lips, took off his hat, ran his fingers along the sweatband inside it, wiped his fingers on his pants, and put his hat back on.

"Here's the deal," he said, "and this is the last of it. I'll give you two dollars a day for a day's work. I don't pay the colored but seventy-five cents, and some of the whites a dollar. But you three look healthy enough, and I need someone that can work a full day. Maybe the boy here I'll have to give less. But you two can put a full day in, I can tell by looking at you."

"Two dollars, huh?" Jane said.

"What I said. Again, colored don't get but seventy-five cents and most whites only a dollar, so that's good money."

"That's not fair," Jane said.

"Ain't nobody said a darn thing about it being fair. Take it or leave it."

I looked at Jane. I knew she had about three or four dollars left in her pocket. It was okay money for twenty-five miles, but not okay money for once we got there. Who knew how long we'd have to look for Strangler, or if we'd ever find him? She studied my face for a moment, sighed, turned, and looked at Tony. He nodded.

She turned back to the man, said, "All right. We'll do it. But I want you to know, the way you're treating those colored people is not fair, and I don't like it."

"Say you don't?"

"I don't," she said.

"Thanks for clearing that up," he said. "It's good to know where the hired help stands."

34

"I'm Big Bill Brady," he said. "And now you work for me. I can give you a ride to the fields in my car, unless your limousine is about to show."

"Don't judge a book by its cover," Jane said. "You'll often

be wrong. And as for a ride, why would we need a ride to the fields and it about to be dark? There's no pea picking can be done when it gets dark."

"'Cause I got barracks for my workers," he said. "This is a big first-class operation. I sell peas to the canning factory over in Lindale."

"Barracks?" I said. "You mean a place to sleep?"

"Yep. It's tidy and it's got a roof on it, and I serve three meals a day. I got sixteen workers, not counting you three."

A man came walking along the street then, a tall skinny fellow. He tipped his hat at us, said, "Hello, Bill," and kept walking.

"How far is this place from here?" Jane said.

"It's a ways," he said. "You couldn't walk it. It's down in the bottoms. Rich land. It'll grow any seed dropped in it, and grow it big. Thing is, I want at least five days work if you come on. Five days, you'll have ten dollars a piece, and you won't be out for a place to stay, or have to sleep under a tree, and you'll have meals you won't have to pay for"—he nodded at our cans on the bench—"and it won't be beans out of a can. My wife cooks pretty good meals. You'll eat and sleep in the barracks, but you'll work a good, long full day for your money and your upkeep."

"End of those five days," Jane said, "you'll bring us back?"

"I will. End of that day, after you've had a nice supper, I'll drive you back into town and let you out right here at this bench. Then you can go your own way. But I need the workers, and my guess is even if you do have a fortune waiting for you on the other end, it's still a good many miles, and you got to depend on a ride to catch, and you'll still need some money till you get there. Who knows, the inheritance might fall through. Another relative with better connections might come out of the woodwork. A tricky lawyer, a crooked judge or law official. I've seen it happen."

I knew he knew we didn't have any inheritance coming, and that he was just buttering us up a little, but he was darn good at it, and I began to think I ought to have some concerns for the inheritance we didn't have coming.

"It's a deal, then," Jane said, "providing Jack and Tony agree."

We agreed.

"All right, then," Big Bill Brady said. "Get in the car."

It probably wasn't smart for us to get in a car with someone we didn't know, and I'd be the first to admit that that is a true consideration. But there was things he had on his side. An offer of money for work. A fellow passed him on the street and knowed him enough to say hello, and would recognize us if our bodies turned up in the pea patch. And there was another thing: what he said about those barracks and square meals was right appealing. I was hungry and tuckered out.

Still, I put my hand in my pocket and got hold of my pocketknife so I could pull it out and pop it open. I kept it there while I sat in the front seat of the car and Jane and Tony sat in the back. I glanced back at Jane, saw she'd pulled one of those cans of beans out of one of our bags, and she had it held in her hand in such a way that I knew if the man up front got to acting funny, she'd bring it down on his head like a ton of bricks.

She grinned at me.

Turning back in the seat, I started watching where we were going. I wanted to have my bearings, have some idea of where we were going to end up, and some idea of how to come back the way we had gone.

We drove for a good hour, I figured, and finally we turned off onto a narrow road that went down deep into the woods. The road was so bad, Big Bill had to drive slow, and I figured I had to, I could jerk the car door open and leap out. I had leaped off a train going faster, so I knew I could handle this.

But Bill didn't do anything, or say anything, so I didn't. He just kept driving, now and again reaching through the open window to adjust his mirror on the side of the car.

The road emptied out into a wide field planted in peas. You could see them in the moonlight, all green and shiny. The trees didn't start up again until the far side of the field. They was just a dark line on the other side.

We turned onto what was nothing more than a trail and began to ride around the field.

"Them's just some of the peas," Big Bill said. "That's just one of the fields. But they all got to get picked so they don't ruin. That's going to be your field."

The car bumped along a little more, and then we saw a long low-slung building on the far side of the field, near the trees. Bill drove directly for that.

When he got to it, he got out of the car quickly, leaving the door open. He pulled a revolver from somewhere, probably from under his seat, and pointed it inside the car. He said,

"I see you with that can of beans in the wing mirror, girl. Why don't you put it down."

Jane dropped the can on the floorboard.

Bill wagged the gun at me. "And I know you got your hand in your pocket there, and I'm thinking pocketknife, 'cause whatever's there ain't big enough to be a gun."

"What about me?" Tony said.

"Hell, boy," Bill said. "You ain't got nothing."

"I hope," Jane said, "that you didn't bring us all the way out here to steal what's in our bags, 'cause you are going to be sorely disappointed."

"Nothing like that," Bill said. "I brought you here to pick peas, just like I said."

"But I'm thinking," Jane said, "not for two dollars a day."

"You're smart," he said.

"Not smart enough," she said.

"No," he said, "not smart enough."

"Will we get a dollar?" Tony asked.

"No," Bill said. "No dollar."

"Same as the colored?" Tony asked.

"Even the colored don't make what I said the colored make," Big Bill said. "And I ain't got sixteen workers neither."

He waved the pistol at me. "Toss that pocketknife on the seat there and get out of the car."

35

As we walked toward the barracks, Big Bill behind us with the pistol, I felt like the world's biggest horse's ass. Being tired and hungry can suck your smarts away sure as a leech on your leg can suck your blood. Right then I felt I couldn't have been any dumber if my head was cut off.

When we got to the barracks, I noted there were no windows, just some trapdoors in the walls that were held shut with long metal rods that ran through them. The rods were fastened to the building with padlocks on either end. There was no light coming through any cracks. Inside it might as well have been the bottom of the ocean.

"Here's your nice barracks," he said. "You can find your place inside."

"We'll be missed," Jane said. "My relatives have plenty of money, and they'll send the law looking. They'll find us, and they'll find you."

"Oh, you don't have to worry about those rich relatives I figure you don't have," Big Bill said. "Or the law either."

He reached in his shirt pocket and pulled out a badge and held it up so we could see it in the moonlight.

It was a sheriff's badge.

"Dang it," Tony said.

"Yeah," Big Bill said. "Dang it. Thing about being sheriff is I pretty much do what I want. I ain't out to hurt you none. I want you to know that. I just want my peas picked, and I ain't got the money to get them picked, least not the way I want. And then there's this: I don't want to pick them myself. And couldn't. Not all those peas."

"I don't figure you actually planted them," Jane said.

"No. I had help."

"Our kind of help?" I said. "Meaning you watched from the sidelines?"

"Now that you mention it, yes."

"You are not much of a lawman, are you?" Jane said.

"Listen here," he said, "times is tough. I'm sheriff, and I don't even have a house to live in. My other property, where I lived, the bank took it. These days, you got to do what you got to do to get along. And these pea patches, that's how I get along. Them and my car is what I got."

"So that makes it all right," Jane said.

"No. But it makes it what it is," he said.

"This ain't just five days, is it?" I said.

"I get through with you here, it'll be more than five days, but I'll let you go when the job's done. And if you're thinking you'll tell someone, don't bother. I'll just say you spent your pay and we didn't get along while you worked here, and you're just saying bad things about me 'cause you're . . . what's the word?"

153

"Try *disgruntled*," Jane said.

"That wasn't what I was looking for," Big Bill said, "but if that means mad as hell, that'll do."

"Close enough," Jane said.

"Step to the left there," Big Bill said.

We did. We had been standing in front of a padlocked door. He got the key out of his pocket with his other hand while he held the gun on us. He unlocked the padlock and pulled it off.

"Go on in," he said.

"I guess," Jane said, "this means we won't be getting those three hot meals a day either."

"Beans," he said, "same as you got in that can in the car."

We went inside and he closed the door. Right away, I knew there were people in there with us. I could hear them breathing. It was the kind of breathing you hear when people are worn out and sleeping. It was the kind of breathing my daddy used to do when he was through with a hard day and nothing had really come of it. There was also a smell about the place—the smell of body odor and chickens. I realized this long building had once been a chicken roost. Probably Sheriff Big Bill had raised chickens before he decided to replace them with folks like us and grow peas.

At the far end of the long building, on the back side, was light. The front might have been tight as a fat lady's corset, but there was a bit of light on the long back wall. It was just a cut of moonlight, thin as a razor, and not that bright, but it showed me someone sitting on the floor with their back to the wall looking at us. I say looking at us, though I couldn't be certain. I only knew whoever it was, was facing our direction.

154

My eyes began to adjust a bit, and now I could see that all along the sides of the building, lying on what looked to be feed sacks, were people. I couldn't tell anything about them, if they were men or women. I could tell that most were big enough that they had to be at least my age.

We walked down between them toward the light. I don't know exactly why we did that, but I guess it's the way people are. We're always looking for the light. At the rear, in the strip of moonlight, we could see who was sitting there now. It was a colored fella, probably our age. He had on overalls. He was awake, and he was looking at us.

"All the room left is back here," he said "There's some space along the wall here, you don't mind sitting with me."

"Of course we don't," Jane said.

"There's some in here won't. They don't want to be by no colored."

"We're all some kind of color," she said.

"Shut up," someone said from the dark. "Bad enough we're here, worse we can't sleep."

We sat down along the wall and spoke quietly.

"We was snookered by the sheriff," Jane said.

"Yeah, he got me a week ago," said the kid. "He promised me a dollar."

"He promised us two," Tony said.

"Your promise was better," said the kid, "but looks like what we got is the same."

"Yep," Jane said. "It does. What's your name?"

"Gasper."

"Gasper?" Jane said.

"That's it."

"That's an odd name."

"Tell me about it. I never did get to ask my mama why she called me that. She died. She got the lung disease."

"I'm sorry," Jane said.

"Me too," Gasper said.

"Is this as bad as it looks?" I said.

"It's worse than it looks. All these folks. They, as you say, was snookered. I was traveling down from Oklahoma looking for work. I got some along the way, and then I got this promise, and it wasn't much, but I thought a roof over my head, meals, that was worth something. Well, I got a roof over my head, but it's not so much. I got a bag to lay down on. There's other bags there for y'all."

"How thoughtful of Sheriff Big Bill," Jane said.

"Yeah, ain't it," Gasper said.

"We're from Oklahoma too," I said. "Around Hootie Hoot."

"I ain't never heard of it," Gasper said. "My mama died and my daddy was already gone. I was living with my grandmother, but she died too. Just got old. I was already doing a man's work, so I thought I'd go down here and do it and be out of the sand. I'm out of it, but I ain't no better."

"We're down this way looking for Jane's relatives," I said. "By the way, I'm Jack, and this is Tony."

"I guess I'm glad to meet you," Gasper said, "but all things considered, I don't know this is such a fine moment for any of us."

"How's it work?" Jane said.

"You mean the job?" Gasper said.

"I mean the slavery," Jane said.

156

"Yeah, ain't that something? I thought my people was through with that. But the way it works is you better get some rest. You'll need it."

"You don't look like you're resting," I said.

"I was just sitting here thinking on how to get out of this situation. But you better rest. Tomorrow, before the sun comes up, he'll come get you, and he's got two other white men with him that's both as big a skunk as he is. No offense meant on the white remark."

"None taken," Jane said.

"Those men work for him and get a cut of the pea sales to the canning factory."

"Looks like it would be cheaper to pay labor instead of overseers," Jane said.

Gasper shook his head. "Nope. He can work us as long as it takes. Those men, all they got to do is stand around with guns, and when the peas get gathered, they run them by truck to Lindale and get paid pretty good money, even for this depression. Good compared to some things, anyhow, and all they got to do is stand around. It's our backs get tired, not theirs. And heck, they even get a cut of the peas. I wish I did. I especially like them crowder peas and the red rippers."

"Don't do that," Jane said, "you're going to make me hungry. They just come get us in the morning and put us to work?"

"Yep," Gasper said. "They take you out to the field, and the men with guns are there. Shotguns. They ain't playing, that's what I'm trying to tell you. I seen a man run for it and they shot him."

"Really?" I said.

"It looked real enough to me," Gasper said. "They shot him and he didn't get up. A couple of them dragged him off and we didn't never see him again. I doubt they've given him an inside job somewhere. He's dead."

"Damn," Jane said.

"Yeah," Gasper said. "Damn. When you get there, you start working right away. You pick peas, fill your bags, and empty them in bushel baskets in the back of a truck at the ends of the rows. There's two trucks. It goes like that until it gets solid dark, then they march you back here, give you some beans, and it starts all over the next day. That one meal is all you get. Did he promise you the three a day?"

"He did," I said. "Can't believe we fell for it."

"Times like this make a person stupid," Gasper said. "Something deep down told me this wasn't a good idea, and I did it anyway."

"We understand that," I said.

For a while we just sat there and felt sorry for ourselves. Then Jane said, "Didn't you say you been thinking on things, like maybe you know a way out?"

"I don't know it's a way out, but there's something I been thinking on trying. I ain't had the courage yet."

"Any of the others in on it?" Jane said.

"No."

"Why did you even mention it to us?" Jane asked.

"'Cause you talk to me and don't mind sitting by me," Gasper said. "Also, I think y'all can run fast, and maybe the others here can't. Most of them are old worn-out men and women that ain't got nothing to look forward to, except

158

maybe this roof and that bowl of beans at the end of the day. They don't like it, and they don't deserve it, but I think maybe they've done given up. Us together, we might do something. One thing I learned is this stuff about how a man has to stand up and make it on his own is all right if you got money and some talent or some luck. But if all you got is two legs and two arms and have to work, it's right tough."

"Amen to that," Jane said.

"What I'm thinking is, on the east side of the field, where we dump some of the peas—and you got to be in the row going that way to dump your bag—there's a swamp. I think that's the way out. On the other side is just woods. They got an old hound dog they can bring into things if they want. It ain't always around, but sometimes they have it. It'll bite too. I seen it bite a man once."

"I don't swim very well," I said.

"Don't need to," Gasper said. "It's about knee-deep, and once you get into it a ways, there's trees everywhere. Still water, but trees to hide behind."

"That doesn't sound like much," I said.

"No, it don't," Gasper said, "but there's a little more to it. Couple days back I was by the swamp, dumping my bag of peas into baskets in the truck, and I noticed something. There was a fishing boat that had floated up. It ain't where we are now, it's on up the rows, but we'll be there in about three days."

"I see where this is going," I said.

"Yeah," Gasper said. "Ain't much to it, really. And it may not even be a boat that's all together. It could be caught up there in roots and vines and have a hole in the bottom. I only seen it from a distance. It probably come loose from along the river somewhere. It looked real worn. It might have been floating around out there for years before it come to rest in them trees. Thing is, though, it's a good trek to get to it, and shotgun blasts travel quick. So my plan is simple: when I get up there even with it, I'm going to go for it, try and push it out in deeper water and make an escape."

"Iffy," I said.

"Yeah, it is," Gasper said. "But I don't know how much longer I can take this."

"Maybe we could all take a look tomorrow, and then we might have some idea about it," Jane said. "Maybe four heads will be better than one."

"Yeah, maybe," Gasper said.

"Forget the boat," Tony said. "Just take the truck."

"What, now?" Gasper said.

"Just jump in the truck and drive off."

"I don't reckon they leave the keys in it," I said.

"Yeah they do," Gasper said. "You see, they start at one end, and when we pick, they keep easing the truck up. They leave the keys in it. When I come up with my bag to dump, I seen the man pulling up and getting out, and I seen the keys. But I didn't think nothing of it 'cause I can't drive."

"I can drive," I said.

"He's the only one of us who can," Jane said. "Tony was about to learn how, and then Papa got the tractor rolled over him."

"I never had nobody to teach me," Gasper said.

"Pa only wanted to teach me so I could do the work he didn't want to do," Tony said.

"That's the truth," Jane said.

"Thing is," Gasper said, "it won't be any easier taking the truck than getting to the boat, 'cause they're right there by the truck."

"Yeah," I said. "But wading in a swamp with a gun pointed at you ain't all that easy of an escape either."

"Way I figure," Gasper said, "ain't none of it any good."

"No," Jane said. "But those two ideas, right now, they're all we got."

36

I didn't sleep so good, 'cause that bag I was lying on wasn't any thicker than a wish and a prayer.

Sheriff Big Bill and another man opened the door and called us out before daylight. I was so sore from that hard ground I could hardly walk. Bill had his revolver in a holster on his hip, and the other man had a shotgun. The man with the shotgun was grinning all the time we came out. He really grinned when Jane came out.

I figured, even by not meaning to, she had already added another fly to the ointment. Her being pretty was something that bad people noticed as much as good, but the bad people didn't have a positive mind-set about the matter.

As we were being shuffled out to the fields, a rooster crowed off in the distance. We were up before him. It was pretty bad when the rooster got to sleep in and we didn't.

When we arrived at the field, it was still not daylight, but by the time we went to the back of a truck and were given bags and sent out into the field, morning light was creeping through the trees like a bloodstain.

Gasper took his picking bag and said to me, "Middle of the day, you're going to get so hungry your belly is going to think your throat is cut. Take a few of the peas and strip them and eat them. Don't let them see you do it, but you'll need to do it. They ain't much, but they'll keep you going. They'll give you water, and sometimes they give you a little bread, but you can't count on it. Only meal you can count on is the beans, and they ain't always good and cooked, and Sheriff and his boys don't mind if there's a bug or two in 'em. But you best eat 'em all, otherwise you'll be so weak you can't get up."

"Thanks," I said.

They put us in some close-together rows, each of us in a different row, though there was someone at your back picking the one behind you. I had Gasper at my back.

I counted and there were ten workers all together, counting us and Gasper. The other six were four men and two women. All of them were old, and a couple of them were Mexican. Probably come across the border looking for work and ended up with this. One of them had the shakes. Gasper said it was because he was a drinker and now he wasn't getting any liquor.

We picked, and off to the east—I knew that because that was where the sun rose—I could see a pickup with two men standing at it. Both of them had shotguns. Behind them I could see the swamp water that ran along the edge of the field, and a ways in back of that were the trees. I tried to see the boat up above it, but couldn't. I hoped it was still there, but the idea of the boat was less and less interesting to me. That didn't make Tony's idea of stealing the truck seem any better, but at least it was an idea that wasn't wet.

Within a couple of hours, my back ached. I hadn't done this kind of work in a while. Maybe it wouldn't have been so bad had there been money and not slavery, and if the hours were reasonable.

After picking until noon, we were allowed to go up to the truck on the east side to get a drink. We took turns with a dipper in a water can. We were allowed two dips, then we were done. The water was warm, but it was water. My clothes were so wet with sweat, it was like I had been wearing them swimming. They let us sit awhile in the shade of the truck, but it was time for us to get up and go before we were any kind of rested.

Maybe that was best. I could hardly move, and the longer I sat, the harder it was to get up.

When I come around in front of the truck, I looked down a ways and saw what Gasper had been talking about. It wasn't much of a boat, and I thought even if we got to it, there were no paddles, and those men could wade after us as fast as we could wade in. It was a plan that hadn't sounded too good to begin with, but now it seemed even worse.

We picked all day, and when night finally came, we picked a little in the dark and unloaded our peas into the baskets. There was only one man at the truck now, and he kept telling us to hurry.

The other man had gone off in the woods, most likely to take care of bathroom business. By the time we were walking across the row again, the man with the shotgun was at our backs, and the other one had come out of the woods and got in the truck and drove it off. As he did, a big bloodhound lifted its head up and stuck it out the window. Another problem with trying to steal the truck. Dogs bite.

They took us to where there was an outhouse and let us go in there one at a time and do our business, with them beating on the door almost the second we were inside, telling us to hurry. It wasn't a thing that lent itself well to a bathroom visit.

Back at the barracks, we went inside, and a little later, Sheriff Big Bill came with a pot of beans and a man with a shotgun. Bill had metal plates, and he passed those out, and then some metal cups. He scooped beans from the pot with a cup, gave us all a plateful. They let us dip some water from a water cooler, and then we had to sit down. We didn't have any spoons, so we ate the beans with our fingers and sucked the juice from the plate by tilting it into our mouths.

The beans were cold and the water was warm. They took up our plates and cups and took the pot and the water with them. They locked the door. The sound of that padlock going into place was like hearing the crack of doom.

Jane sat down against the wall where we'd been the night before and said, "Home, sweet home."

37

Sitting in the barracks, our backs against the wall, we talked some, all except Jane. She just kept staring at the crack in the wall, and at the little bit of moonlight and starlight coming in through it.

Eventually the talk died down, and we were getting ready to settle in, when Jane said, "I saw that boat. I don't think it's such a good idea. They'd shoot your head off before you got to it, and if you did get to it, they could still wade out to you faster than you could push it off. And if there aren't any paddles in the boat, you couldn't make any real time. You'd be better off just trying to slosh through the water. And you know what I saw out there?"

"What?" Gasper said. "A snake?"

"I saw a couple of them too, but what I meant was I saw an alligator. I don't like alligators, and I can say that without ever having any kind of personal relationship with one. And I don't want my first visit with them to be about lunch, and me being the lunch."

"An alligator?" Tony said.

"Yes, sir," Jane said. "An alligator."

"Count me out on that plan," Tony said. "I'd rather pick peas."

"What I'm wondering," Jane says, "is what happens to us when all the peas are picked. He says no one would believe us, but I think maybe he might think someone would."

"You mean he might hurt us?" I said.

"I was thinking something a little beyond hurt," she said. "Obviously, he's not what one would call a fine and upstanding representative of the law. I think he would shoot us, and I think if he didn't, his men would. Gasper already said they killed a man, and we have no way of knowing if there are others. Dead is easier than having to deal with us telling what happened to us, even if it is hard to believe."

"I figure we got a couple weeks of pea picking just in this field," Gasper said. "I think he's got other fields."

"I hear you," Jane said, "but I'm not that fond of pea picking, and I don't want to keep eating beans."

"It's better than eating dirt," Gasper said.

"It is," Jane said, "but if I'm dead I won't taste the dirt. Those beans I got to taste, and I tell you, I'm really tired of them. And let me tell you another thing. I don't like going to the bathroom, then having to eat beans with my fingers. You see where I'm going with this?"

"I just didn't think about that part," said Gasper. "I didn't want to. I wish you hadn't brought it up."

"Yes, but I have," Jane said. "I've thought on the second plan, Tony's plan."

"And?" Tony said.

"I'm going to say this, Gasper," Jane said, "and don't take offense, but it's a better plan than yours."

"I ain't offended," Gasper said.

"That said," Jane said, "it isn't any good either."

"So what now?" I said.

"You see that crack where the light is coming in?" she asked.

We all agreed that we did.

"It's wide enough to get fingers through," she said.

"So," Gasper said.

"So, nothing for sure," Jane said, "but you see that dust on the floor there, piled up on the dirt? That's termite work. They've been working on that spot, maybe a lot of other spots. But this spot I can see, and the way I figure it, Jack here, who is a strapping young man, or you, Gasper, might be able to get their fingers through the crack and pull on it, see if the boards will loosen any."

"If I pull," I said, "I'm just going with the way the nails are driven in."

"Let me say that different," Jane said. "See if you can get a handhold of some sort, and push."

Sometimes you hear an idea, and you think, that's not

much of an idea, it's too simple. You been thinking about splashing through water, stealing a boat, or maybe trying to take the truck and run, fight off a bloodhound and dodge shotgun pellets, and then someone says something simple, and you think, that can't work, there ain't nothing to it. But another part of you says, you know, maybe you been over-thinking this thing.

I stuck my fingers through. I could only get two through it, the two closest to my thumb. I did that and grabbed with them and pushed with my palm. It was kind of like trying to turn a car over.

"That isn't working so good," I said.

"Here," Gasper said. "Let me try with you."

He got a lower place in the crack, which ran from the top of the building to the bottom, and pushed. That didn't move anything either.

Tony laid on his back and put his feet against the board and we all pushed. There was a squeak of nails.

"I think it loosened a bit," Gasper said.

We all stopped and waited, thinking that squeak might bring someone running, but it didn't. Way we felt right then, it was a chance worth taking. The sheriff thought he had us locked in good, and that might be to our advantage. He might not have too swell an eye on things right then, and if that was the case, we had a chance at getting away. Wasn't but one way to find out.

Jane got up and came over and put her palms on the board, and we pulled our fingers out of the crack and we all leaned against it, with Tony pushing with his feet. It didn't squeak again. Then I felt something in the dark. It was the other folk in there. They had come over to stand by us.

"We can all push," said one of the two women. "We ain't got much strength by ourselves, but together we might be able to do something."

They scrambled about, finding a place for their hands, trying not to step on Tony as he pushed with his legs.

So we all pushed.

The nails squeaked.

That made us pause. But only for a moment. No one came to stop us. We were desperate, and we were committed. So we pushed some more. One of the boards loosened near the bottom. It was too narrow for anyone to get out there, and it was still hooked solid at the top, but we kept pushing at it, and pretty soon it popped out. We stopped then, listened.

No one came running around to shoot us.

A dog didn't bark.

"They figure we're so good and locked-in," said one of the men, "they don't even keep a close guard."

"Yeah," said the woman who had spoken before. "We all just give up. But we weren't all together on things."

"Don't talk it to death," Jane said. "Push."

We did, and this time the next board popped off and we could wiggle through. Tony was first, and then the women and the men, followed by Jane, with me and Gasper bringing up the rear.

When I looked out at the others, they were running into the woods like deer. All that togetherness hadn't lasted long, which is pretty much the way of things. People only come together when there's no other choice; the rest of the time they think they're free birds and don't need anybody. Until next time.

The four of us started out toward the woods, and when we did, suddenly headlights hit us, and then we heard Big Bill Brady yell, "Stop, or I'll shoot!"

38

I didn't know where he came from, or why he hadn't heard us before, unless he was sleeping sound in his truck, but when we came out from the back of the house and our group scattered to the woods, the truck lights came on, and Big Bill opened the door and stepped out.

He had a shotgun, and he jerked it to his shoulder and fired. The blast went by us and the shot rattled around in the woods back there, but it didn't hit us.

"He ain't playing none," Gasper said. "Run for it!"

We broke away from where he was shooting, but that carried me and Jane and Tony and Gasper into a section of woods where there was water. Soon as we hit it, we had to slow down. It came up to our knees pretty fast. We hadn't even known it was like that back there.

Tony and Jane were ahead of me. I looked back. Gasper had fallen behind. Big Bill stood at the edge of the water. We were moving between the trees, but were still within gunshot range.

The shotgun roared and I could hear pellets slapping trees and sprinkling in the water, and I saw Gasper twist and go down. I admit, for a moment I thought about charging onward, leaving Gasper. I admit that, because Jane and Tony were ahead of me, and I feared losing them. But it was only for a moment. Gasper was one of us, and I couldn't leave him behind. I turned and splashed back toward him, going fast as the water would allow.

The shotgun was a double-barrel, and that had been two shots, both triggers pulled at once. I saw Big Bill snap it open and I glimpsed the empty casings popping out of it and then I saw him pull fresh shells from his pants pocket. I grabbed Gasper and got him up and we kind of stumbled together toward a tree that was twisted with moss and vines. I got us behind that, and as we went onward, I tried to stay in line with it.

Behind us, Big Bill had entered the water and was coming after us, cussing and sloshing along.

"Can you run?" I said.

"If I could run," Gasper said, "I'd be running."

"You got to try."

"I'm trying. You think I don't want to run? You think I'm not trying? I'm hit pretty good."

I took us out into the darker part of the woods, and when

I looked back, Big Bill was coming right for us. I was glad the hound wasn't with him.

As we sloshed along, I found that though the water looked shallow, it was pretty deep. It wasn't long before it was over our knees again. One of Gasper's legs wasn't working, and I was holding him up as best as I could.

There was splashing behind me. I looked back. Big Bill was gaining on us, but I kept weaving us in between trees so he couldn't get off a good shot. I saw him raise the gun to his shoulder once, but we got behind a tree and he didn't fire.

I looked around for Jane and Tony but didn't see them. Good, they had gotten away.

"Let me go," Gasper said. "Doing like this, he's just going to get us both. You can get away."

"I'm sticking," I said.

We went between some trees, and then there was a large patch of moonlight on the water, and we could see the image of the moon there. It was like it was floating in the swamp. I heard a splash and saw the wet darkness ripple.

I stopped moving. Something swam right by us, mostly under the water, but not completely. It wasn't something small. It wasn't a fish. And it wasn't a snake.

Turning, I saw Big Bill wading into the water, pointing the shotgun at us.

"Looks like you're about to end your employment," he said.

I flinched, halfclosed my eyes, waiting for the shot.

And it came.

But I didn't fall.

I looked at Gasper. I still had my arm around his shoulder. He was still standing.

Big Bill wasn't, however. He was being knocked backwards by something in the water. The shotgun had gone off and scattered pellets in front of him and all across the moonlit water, but not at us.

He dropped the gun and screamed. It was the kind of scream that crawled up my back and went along my neck and settled at the top of my head. He went backwards swiftly, and when he did his hat went flying. Something rose up between his legs and bit him there.

It was an alligator.

The next instant the alligator went under with him and the water churned. Once, the body of Big Bill broke the water, still in the alligator's jaws, and then he went down again and didn't come back up. The water was churning, and I thought in the moonlight it looked a little darker, like something was leaking up from the bottom to the top.

"Come on," I said. "We got to move."

We waded across the water, and it got deep. I wasn't a swimmer, so Gasper helped me, using one leg and one arm to swim. He said, "You got to move one of your arms and both your legs."

"I'm holding on to you," I said.

"That's why I said one arm. I can't use my right leg, so you got to help. Kick, for heaven's sake."

We halfway argued all the way across the water, to where the trees grew thick and the water was shallow once more. After slipping down a few times, we managed to finally get up, and with my arm around Gasper, we moved deeper into the woods, where the moon didn't shine. Finally we came to a low tree covered in moss. It had some good limbs, so I climbed up in it, held my hand down, and helped Gasper up.

There wasn't enough light to really see. We mostly did all this by feel. We weren't far above the water, but at least we were out of it. A bullfrog bleated and crickets sawed at their legs, and somewhere a night bird called.

"You saved my life, Jack," Gasper said.

"You ain't taking good notes, Gasper—that was you who helped me swim across that sinkhole. I haven't never really swam before, just paddled."

"Trust me, Jack, what you did, I don't call that swimming."

39

When morning came we were both awake. We had been too uncomfortable and scared to sleep. The sunlight slipped in through the trees and warmed us up a bit and allowed us to see, even though there was some shade from the trees and the moss. I thought about Jane and Tony but had no idea which direction they had gone, or how to even look for them.

We hadn't gone that far from the farm, but we were hid up good in the swamp trees. We couldn't go back the way we had come because of Big Bill's men. I didn't know for sure they were back there, but they could be. Going forward seemed the only choice, and it wasn't a good one. The swamp stretched out for a great distance. And it was full of all manner of bad things, from snakes and alligators to thorns and deep water. Not to mention all the diseases you could get.

During the night, we had been bitten by mosquitoes. I had welts on the back of my neck and on my shoulders. They had bit me right through my clothes. There were still mosquitoes this morning, and Gasper claimed they were big enough to straddle a turkey flat-footed.

I also discovered that two leeches had nestled into my private parts, and I had to reach down in my pants and pull them loose and toss them away. When I did, my hands came away bloody.

Gasper had to do the same. He had one on his foot, right above his shoe top. He didn't have socks, so it was dug in good.

When he finished tossing them, his hands were bloody too.

"I feel kind of sick," he said.

"Not feeling too spry myself," I said.

I looked out through the trees, and now with the sunlight there, I could see the sinkhole, the deep part we had swam across, but I didn't see any gators. I did see Big Bill's hat, however. It was floating in some moss on the far side.

"What now?" Gasper said.

"How's your leg?"

"Not so good."

"Let me see."

He pulled up his pants leg. His calf was red and had pocks and pimples from the shotgun pellets. I figured the blast had skimmed and skipped across the water, slowing them down.

"You're hit, but not bad," I said. He just caught you a little."

"It feels like a lot on this end."

I could see that the buckshot hadn't done a lot of damage. But the wound was starting to be infected. It wouldn't take long before that became a problem, especially with us being in the dirty swamp.

We climbed down out of the tree, went back into the water. I helped him along. The water stayed shallow as we went. I watched for alligators but didn't see any. A big old water moccasin about the width of an inner tube from a bicycle tire and about as long and thick as my arm swam by, but it didn't pay us any mind.

I don't know how long we went along like that, but it was a good ways. The farm was no longer visible. All there was now was lots of water and trees growing up out of the swamp. I had no idea where we were. For all we knew, the swamp could go like that for miles and miles. I hated it that we had gotten separated from Jane and Tony, and I figured they was as lost as us. The idea of something happening to them was overwhelming. But there was no way to look for them right then, and I had no idea which direction they had taken. At least for the time being, it was more important to take care of Gasper, and doing that didn't allow me a lot of room for anything else, even worrying about my friends.

After a while Gasper's limp got worse. I tried to carry him on my back, but he and I were about the same size, and I might as well have been trying to carry a water buffalo.

Resting more often, we finally made it to where the water got thinner and the land got more solid. Eventually we were on dry land. We laid out on it and rested until the sun was almost down.

When I got up, Gasper couldn't.

He pulled up his pants leg and I took a look. It was swollen and was still red, and now there were black streaks under his skin. There were a few pellets that had worked their way to the surface. He pinched a couple of those out.

"Your hands aren't clean," I said. "Don't."

"It hurts something awful, Jack. I don't think I can go on. This time, you got to listen. You got to leave me."

"Don't be an idiot."

"Why the hell would you stay here with me?"

"Because we're friends."

"We don't know each other that well," he said.

"After what we been through together, don't we?"

"Yeah," he said. "Yeah. You're right. We're friends. I ain't never had a white friend before."

"And I ain't never had a gunshot friend, so that makes us even. You can't go on, maybe I should look and see if I can find help. I'll be back, though, you can count on it."

"I believe you."

I gave him a pat on the back. "Hold on, buddy. I'll see what I can find."

40

I went through the woods, making sure to stop and figure out how to find my way back to Gasper. I made a few marks with sticks, by breaking them off and poking them up in the ground, and I scooped out some dirt with my heels, mounding it up. I had me a kind of map, that way. Something I felt I could follow back.

The day was hot, and I was feeling sticky and weak, so I sat down on the ground for a rest. When I looked up, the biggest, ugliest dog I've ever seen was peeking out at me from between some trees. He was bigger than a wolf, and his fur was all twisted up and had briars and such in it, and he looked blue. He had a head about the size of a hog's head, and he looked strong enough to drag me off into the woods and eat me and make me like it.

I said, "Dog, if you're going to eat me, then get it over with. I'm hungry, thirsty, and tuckered out. I ain't got no fight left in me."

When I spoke, the dog stuck out his tongue and dropped his head, and came out of the trees wagging his tail.

"You just look like a bad dog, don't you."

He came to me. I was still too tired to stand. I reached out and patted him on the head. When I pulled my hand back, it stunk like a dead skunk.

"Whoa. You are stinky, aren't you?"

I got up and started walking again. Stinky walked with me. I didn't know where he had come from or if he belonged to someone, but I won't lie, I was glad for company.

Coming to a fork in the trail, I turned right, and the dog didn't go with me. He whined and barked. When I looked back, he was standing right where the trail forked.

"What's with you, Nasty?" I said.

He barked at me.

I went back and gave his stinky head a pat. He started down the fork to the left, turned and looked at me, and barked.

I got it. He lived the other way. And if he lived with someone, that was the way I ought to go.

"All right," I said, "Lead the way, Nasty."

He turned and bolted down the trail, and I went after him.

41

I smelled fish cooking, and then the dog ran up over a rise, and when I came down on the other side, I saw a clearing in the trees, and there was a cabin there with a couple of old pickups sitting out beside it. Smoke was coming out the chimney, and there were people on the porch.

One of the people was a colored man in overalls and lace-up boots. He saw Nasty coming before he saw me, and then when he saw me, the others on the porch looked. As we got closer, I saw that the others were Jane and Tony. I was so excited and happy my heart skipped a beat.

Jane jumped up off the porch and ran out to meet me, threw her arms around me, and kissed me on the cheek.

"We was afraid you got shot, or drowned, or a snake got you."

"Nearly got shot. Nearly drowned. Saw a snake. Alligator ate Big Bill."

"Wow," Jane said. "Where's Gasper?"

"He got shot and couldn't walk. I left him to look for help."

The big colored man, who was even bigger close up, came out to me and said, "You say someone was shot?"

I explained what had happened.

"You should grab something to eat," he said, "and then we can go."

"I can't leave him there while I eat. We got to get him now."

The colored man, who told me his name was Junior, went to the back of his house and came back with a wheelbarrow.

"We'll tote him in this," Junior said.

"Thanks, Mr. Junior."

"You're welcome."

"Hadn't been for your dog, I wouldn't have found you."

"That's not my dog."

"No?"

"I just let him stay around. He come up one day, been here ever since."

I started leading the way and the others followed.

It was a long way back, and when we found Gasper, he was worse. He had a fever and was talking out of his head. I got hold of his feet and Junior got his shoulders, and we lifted him into the wheelbarrow.

The ground was soft, and that made it tough going with the wheelbarrow, but Junior didn't seem to mind. He acted like he could do that all day.

Nasty trotted along just ahead of us, as if he was an official guide.

It was late afternoon by the time we got back to Junior's house, and I was starved. While Junior and Jane took Gasper inside, I sat on the porch and picked at a bony fish that tasted about as good as anything I'd ever ate. When I finished up I went inside. Gasper was stretched out on the bed on his stomach, and Junior had cut his pants leg open with a knife. He was heating the knife in a candle flame when I went in. When it was clean by fire, he poured some whiskey from a bottle over it, then poured some on Gasper's legs. Gasper jumped and said something that didn't make any sense. He was still out of his head.

Junior took a swig of the whiskey, said, "You two going to have to hold him."

I got his shoulders and Jane got his left ankle, where just above it, in the calf, was the wound.

"Young'n," Junior said to Tony, who was standing in the doorway, "you come over here and sit on his good leg."

Tony did just that.

Junior said, "Now, he's going to scream, but don't let him go."

And Junior went to work with the knife.

Gasper had good lungs. He screamed so loud and so long, when we was finished, my ears hurt.

Junior put the buckshot he dug out of Gasper's leg into a bowl on a table beside the bed. He poured more whiskey on the leg when he finished, drank a bit for himself, then wrapped the leg.

We rolled Gasper on his back, and within a moment, he was asleep. Junior touched his forehead. "Fever done broke. Figured it would, soon as I got that lead out of him."

We went out on the porch and let Gasper sleep. Junior

gave some scraps to Nasty and had us tell all that had happened to us. Jane told him, and managed not to gussy it up with a lie.

"No one is going to miss Sheriff Big Bill Brady," Junior said. "Unless maybe he's got a dog. It's good his nonsense is over with."

"Thing is," Jane said, looking over at the sleeping Gasper, "Gasper has no place to go. I don't want to leave him, but we're on a mission. And well, frankly, they ain't gonna let a colored go where we go."

"I know that," Junior said. "I know that every day. That's why I live up here in these woods, where white folks can't tell me what to do and when to do it. Ain't nobody can."

"Maybe we ought to ask Gasper what he wants to do," I said. "It ain't right to make a decision for him."

"It might not be right," Junior said, "but with that leg he ain't going nowhere for a spell, and don't need to have a choice about it. But what did you mean about a mission, girl?"

She explained to him about Strangler and the gangsters. She told it straight, but it sounded like a lie, it was so wild.

"That's some situation," Junior said.

"I know how it sounds," I said. "But it's real."

"I reckon it's true," Junior said. "Though I get this feeling that you, girl, you might stretch the blanket a little. You got some storyteller in you, which is sometimes a word for liar."

"Now and again," she said, "even a true story needs a little something to spice it up."

42

"Now," Junior said, handing me the keys. "That ole pickup ain't much, but it'll run. I just don't know for how long. You can take it and go find your man, and when you get through, you can bring the truck back if it's still running."

I got in behind the wheel, and Jane and Tony went around to the other door and slid onto the seat, Jane in the middle. Junior was holding my door open. Nasty was sitting on the ground wagging his tail.

"What's that dog's name?" I said. "I been calling him Nasty."

"Name?" Junior said, glancing back at the dog. "He ain't got no name. I just call him Dog. But Nasty will do. It fits. He stinks."

"Thanks, Junior," I said. "You'll watch Gasper?"

"He'll be fine," Junior said. "His fever is broke, and he'll wake up hungry and thirsty, you can count on that."

"He don't have a home or no people, besides us," I said.

"He can stay here long as he likes," Junior said. "I could use the company. Here. You going to need a few dollars."

He gave me five dollars in coins.

"You can't do that, Junior," I said.

"Yes I can," Junior said.

I took the money and gave it to Jane.

"Not many people would help strangers like this," I said.

"I'm not many people, son," he said, "and the way I figure it, you ain't either. I mean, didn't the girl say you folks was on a mission? That makes you special, don't it? Besides, I kept the good truck. This one goes to pieces, it's no big loss. I was going to sell it, but I figure I wouldn't get much for it anyway. So I'm not being as nice as you think."

"If you say so," I said.

"Watch your hands," Junior said, and closed the door.

A moment later, I was driving the truck up the little road that led out to where Junior told me I should go.

As we rode along, Jane said, "We're like Odysseus."

"Who?"

"Odysseus. The Romans called him Ulysses."

"Doesn't ring a bell."

"He was an ancient traveler who went to war, and then, after ten years of it, he decided to go home. On his way he ran into all kinds of problems, and it didn't look like he was going to make it, but he got through them and finally did go home. Of course, he had to put a giant's eye out with a sharp stick and kill a bunch of people, but he made it."

"We aren't going home. We left home."

"So we did. Well, maybe it's more like we're Jason and the Argonauts. I'll be Jason and you be somebody on the boat."

"I have no idea what you're talking about," I said.

"She reads a lot," Tony said.

"Jason took a boat with heroes on it and went in search of the Golden Fleece."

"Did he find it?"

"He did," she said. "Point is, he left home, did a great deed, got the fleece, went back home."

"Are we going back home?" I asked.

"I'm not," she said.

"Me neither," I said. "So how's that like Jason and the whatevers?"

"Argonauts. You're missing the point. We are having a great adventure. I'm speaking symbolically again."

"As you noted, I quit school before that lesson."

"Oh yeah," she said, grinning. "I did say that, didn't I. Well. It's true. But still, we're having an adventure."

"Even if we are, we may not be in time to help this Strangler. He could have been dead for days now."

"Could be," she said, "but sometimes it's just about the quest."

"Strangler might think it's about us telling him two gangsters who don't like that he took their stolen money are going to kill him. So for Strangler, it's not just the quest."

"That's an excellent point," Jane said.

We rode on through the late afternoon until we came to the edge of Tyler. We stopped and got a dollar's worth of gas at a station; then we stopped at a barbecue joint and got some sandwiches. We took them outside by the building, sat on the steps, and ate them.

While we were eating, Tony got up and went over to look at a poster on a telephone pole near the street.

"Ain't *Strangler* spelled like this?" Tony said.

We got up and went over to look at the poster. It was for a carnival. It said, COME DEFEAT OUR MAN AND MAKE SOME MONEY! COME BATTLE THE UNDEFEATED STRANGLER NUGOWSKI! Then there was a painted picture of him that made him look a little like a redheaded movie star.

Underneath, it said there was a carnival that night, and it wasn't actually in Tyler, but in Lindale. That was where Pretty Boy said the train would go if we didn't get off. It was where Big Bill took his peas to be canned. I went inside the barbecue joint and asked for directions to Lindale. It wasn't all that far. We got in the truck and I drove us out of there.

"What luck," I said.

"No luck to it," Jane said. "We're looking for him. We know he's in the area. His name is Strangler and he beats people up in carnivals."

"It's still lucky," I said. "We might never have seen that poster. Good job, Tony."

"I liked it. It was bright colored," Tony said.

As we drove along, we saw a lot of the posters on telephone and lamp poles, and even two big billboards talking about the carnival. Plastered across the billboards in big letters was Strangler's name, and how he would take on all comers.

"It's like Bad Tiger and Timmy got a map straight to him," I said.

"Yeah," Jane said, "he might as well paint a bull's-eye on his forehead and send them telegrams. What I want to know is why a thief that's supposed to be hiding from gangsters is

187

working in a carnival, just like nothing ever happened. What is he thinking?"

"Maybe the answer is simple," I said.

"And what would that be?" Jane said.

"He's an idiot."

43

It was late afternoon when we got to Lindale, and I had to drive around and ask a couple of people before someone could tell me where the carnival was going to take place. Turned out it was out near the Lindale canning factory, and that made me think of peas and Sheriff Big Bill.

When we got there, the carnival was setting up for the night. There were people pulling ropes for tents, and there were people putting together stands for places where you tossed balls at bowling pins or tried to flip rings over bottles, and there were carnival rides going up.

I parked the truck on one side of the highway and we went over to the carnival.

When we were on the lot, a man by a Ferris wheel, who looked like his last bath had been taken about the time of his birth came over to us. He walked like he had one leg in a ditch, and the other was short.

"You ain't supposed to be here till tonight," said the carny. "You could get hurt around here before then, things going up and all."

Jane eyed one of the rides not far from the Ferris wheel. It was some kind of ride that looked as if it would swing way out and high and then swing back close to the ground. It was fastened down by ropes and stakes. A couple of men were positioning and tightening bolts that held the ride in place. She said, "Looks to me like we could get hurt tonight, way those bolts are being fastened. They could come loose and throw the whole lot of the riders out there in the street, not to mention puncturing them to death with all those spokes, dropping the seats on them. I'll tell you now, I'm not going to ride that stuff."

"Then don't," said the carny, "it's no skin off my nose."

"We're looking for Strangler," she said. "I'm the captain of his fan club, and he promised an interview for our newsletter. We send it out to thousands."

"He's got a fan club?" the carny said.

"Oh yeah," she said. "He's modest, and probably didn't tell you about it. And I'm going to tell you something I shouldn't, 'cause it might take away from how you feel about him having a fan club. But I'm his cousin."

"Cousin?"

"That's right. Truth is, he hired me to come up with the

club, but then it caught on. Who knew? But the main thing is, that interview should promote the carnival in the next town, wherever that might be."

"Atlanta, Texas."

"Good. Now, where is he?"

"Do you really know Strangler?"

"Boy, do I," Jane said.."All right. I'm not his cousin, and there's no fan club."

"I didn't think so," he said.

"Can I speak to you privately?" she said.

"I suppose so."

Jane walked off with the carny and whispered something and came back to join us. The carny, looking a little stunned, went back to the rickety rides.

"I got directions to Strangler's trailer," she said.

"What did you tell him?" I said.

"That I was pregnant with Strangler's baby."

"And he believed you?"

"It's a better story than the fan club one."

Strangler's trailer was a colorful one with a painting of him on the side. In the painting he had on wrestling shorts and shoes and he was bare-chested and well muscled. He had bright red hair.

The door to the trailer was open, and we could see Strangler sitting inside on a stool reading a comic book. He had on wrestling shorts, wrestling shoes, and a big gray sweatshirt.

Jane knocked on the side of the trailer, "Knock, knock, Mr. Strangler."

Strangler looked up. He resembled the painting on the

side of the trailer enough you could tell it was him, but he had gone a little to fat. His red hair was touched with gray around the ears.

"Who are you?" he said, without getting up.

"We've come to see you don't get killed by a couple of gangsters," Jane said. "Do Bad Tiger and Timmy ring a bell?"

Strangler tossed the comic on the floor. "Come in," he said.

We went inside. There was a couch and a chair, and through an open door I could see a bed.

"What do you know about them guys?" he said.

"What we know," said Jane, "is that they have guns, they are mean, they don't like you, and they want some money back."

"They do, huh?"

"Listen here," Jane said. "We know why you stole it, and we get it. We do. The money, that's not any of our business, not with what you had in mind about your daughter, but they really are serious."

"I ain't got no daughter," Strangler said.

"No?" I said.

He shook his head. "I told them that so my reasons for stealing the money would be better than theirs. I just wanted the money."

"You lied to a couple of gangsters to feel better about yourself?" Jane said.

I was thinking this was exactly what Jane did all the time. She'd rather climb a tree and lie than stand on the ground and tell the truth.

"Yeah. I didn't want to just be a criminal. I'm no criminal."

"Actually," Jane said, "you are the definition of a criminal. You stole money from a bank."

"I know, but I mailed it back. I mailed it back the second day after it was stolen. It took four good-sized boxes. I used the address on the money bags. I sent it from a post office in some little town. I forget the name."

"You seem pretty open about it," I said.

"If you know I had the money, and you know Bad Tiger and Timmy, what's the use lying?"

Okay, he wasn't exactly like Jane.

"Well," Jane said. "You may not see yourself as a criminal, but Bad Tiger and Timmy are criminals, and they see you as one. A crook that took their money. They want it back, and then they want to shoot you. They'll do it. We saw Timmy kill a man."

"That would be Buddy," Strangler said. "He was hit in the robbery. And pretty bad."

"Did you shoot anyone?" I asked.

He shook his head. "I was outside in the car. I was the driver. A bank guard shot Buddy. We hadn't no more than driven out of there with the loot than Timmy was looking at Buddy like he had to go. He didn't want to play nursemaid, drag him around. I could see it in his eyes. I was certain of it."

"Good call," Jane said. "He shot him, all right, and you're next. We found you easy, and so will they. I'm surprised they haven't already. They're bound to show eventually."

"I figure the same," Strangler said. "My guess is they didn't find me 'cause the carnival has been in Missouri and Arkansas. This is the first week we been in Texas. So if they been in East Texas, they been having to wait on me."

"It's not exactly sneaky," Jane said, "to go back to your old line of work in a trailer with your name and likeness on the side of it."

"I ain't running. I sent the money back. I'm no criminal."

"Yeah," Jane said. "You keep saying that."

"I'm through running," Strangler said. "I'm just going to hit people in the ring."

"And those bad boys are going to shoot you," she said, "and when they find out you gave the money back, they're going to shoot you a lot."

"Let them," Strangler said. "I don't care. I ain't running. I gave the money back. I just got sideways for a time there. This Great Depression, as they call it, it got to me. Not having any money and thinking my future wasn't nothing but twisting people in knots and throwing them around. What do I do when I get old? So I got in with some bad people who wanted my muscle. I guess I'd seen too many gangster movies. My mama didn't raise me that way, and I come to that conclusion after we robbed that bank and I saw Buddy take a bullet. We could have killed some of them citizens. I decided it was better to starve. Thanks for trying to help me, but you kids go away. . . . Wake him up."

Tony was asleep on the couch. He had sort of wadded up there and gone right out.

"We've had a rough few days," Jane said. "All because we were coming here to help you."

"That was some of it," I said. "Don't forget the adventure part. Speaking symbolically, of course."

"Oh, go to hell," Jane said, and went out of the trailer.

"She likes you," Strangler said.

"You think?"

"Oh yeah. Can't say how much, but the ones you irritate like that, they like you. They got to like you to get that mad."

"No daughter, huh?" I said.

"Nope," he said. "Made it up."

44

I woke Tony and pulled him off the couch, and we caught up with Jane as she was leaving the carnival lot. The carny we had first spoke to crossed our path on the way out.

He said, "He going to treat you right?"

"No," Jane said, pausing. "I don't believe he is."

"I'm sorry," the carny said. "That isn't very stand-up."

"No," Jane said, "it isn't."

"I know it don't help much, but here," said the carny, and gave her a handful of tickets. "These will get you and your friends in, and give you all the rides you want."

"Thanks," said Jane, and she stuffed them in her pants pocket, headed across the street to where the truck was parked.

When we were all in the truck, I said, "I didn't mean to make you mad back there."

"It's all right," she said. "It isn't you. I figured it was going to be like in a picture show where we save someone's life, and his kid gets her foot fixed, and so on. I was expecting a happy ending. Now he'll just get shot and nobody's foot got fixed."

"None to fix," I said.

"That's what's disappointing," Jane said. "Strangler is just like you said. He's a big idiot. Let's get out of here. He's made his bed, now he can lie in it. Let's go back to Tyler."

"We going to look for your relatives now?" I said.

Jane sighed. "About that. We don't really have any relatives here in East Texas."

"We don't?" Tony said.

"No, we don't," Jane said. "I made that up."

"That ain't right, Jane," said Tony. "I knew that, I'd have stayed with that nice lady."

"I wanted us to all go together," Jane said. "I wanted there to be a place we were going."

"That's pretty low, Jane," I said.

"I know," Jane said. "I'm pretty low."

"You're the worst sister ever," Tony said.

"I'm sure someone can find someone worse," Jane said, "but certainly I'll be getting no rewards for my sisterly manners."

I stopped at a store between Lindale and Tyler with a Coca-Cola machine out front. Jane gave me three nickels, and I used them to get us each a Coca-Cola. We sat on the curb and drank them. Across the street, we could see a billboard

195

with Strangler's name on it. This one also had his picture, same one that was on the side of his trailer.

"They probably been all over East Texas looking for him," I said, "and Strangler has been out of town. But a carnival ain't hard to follow. Might as well be a brass band. If they're going to catch up with him, this would be the place."

"If they're smart," Jane said, "they haven't been following him at all. They know the carnival is going to come through this area eventually, so all they got to do is hole up and wait, and it's all over but the dirt in the face." She took a big swig of her Coca-Cola. "Dang it," she said. "We ought to go back and talk to him again. Get him to run or go to the cops. We can't just leave him, and us knowing what's going to happen. We got to convince him."

"Well, we got carnival tickets," Tony said.

45

It was nighttime when we got to the carnival, and it was shiny with lights and metal rides reflecting light. It was so bright you couldn't see the sky. The air was thick with the smells of hot dogs, cotton candy, and popcorn.

We hadn't no more than given our tickets and gone inside, when we saw Bad Tiger and Timmy. They didn't see us. They were across the way, walking. They both looked rough, like they hadn't changed their clothes in days. They each had a growth of beard, and they had a slump to their walk, like their feet hurt and their souls were no fresher.

Even though I'd been half expecting them to show up, my jaw still dropped. On some level, I think I figured they'd given it all up and we'd never see them again. Or that there wasn't any chance of us showing up at the same time. But there they were.

They were wandering between gaming stands and stacks of cheap teddy bear prizes. We saw them walk in front of the freak show tent with crude paintings of freaks on the sides, bearded women and pinheads and wolf boys and so on. Barkers were beckoning to them, calling out to "Come and give it a try." They didn't break stride. Like us, they were on a mission.

They were going in the opposite direction of Strangler's trailer, which meant they were using guesswork. After a moment, they passed out of our sight.

I caught Jane's shoulder, and she said, "Yeah, I saw them."

Tony said, "I can run around to Strangler's trailer. I can warn him."

"You're nothing but a kid," Jane said.

"Yeah," Tony said, "but I'm a kid that can run fast."

The words were no sooner out of his mouth than he was gone.

We waited there, nervous as long-tailed cats in a room full of rocking chairs. Time went by and the rides circled and swung and dipped and rose, and people yelled and screamed as they did. The carnival ride we were standing next to vibrated like a drunk man about to fall down.

After enough time passed to have planted a crop, harvested it, and sold it on the edge of the street, we saw Tony running toward us. He was all sweated up and he was gasping for air. He stopped in front of us, bent over, and held his side.

"Run all the way there," he said, "and run all the way back."

"We can figure that," Jane said. "What about Strangler?"

"He wasn't there."

"Dang it," Jane said.

And then we heard over a loudspeaker, "Come one, come all! Strangler Nugowski will take on anyone! Prize money twenty-five dollars green American. Come one, come all! Take on Strangler and prove yourself a man! Come one, come all!"

"Oh great," Jane said. "Bad Tiger and Timmy might as well be wolves and Strangler a pork chop."

We went swiftly toward the voice that kept repeating the challenge. We finally ended up in a crowd around a boxing ring raised above the ground maybe five feet. There were steps that led up to it, and right then we saw Strangler jerk off his sweatshirt and go up the steps, like any man going off to work. Some people in the crowd cheered, some booed. He tossed the sweatshirt out of the ring and onto the ground.

Pushing through the crowd, we got yelled at, and threatened, and Jane even got pinched. She slapped a man so hard on the side of the head he went to his knees. He looked up at her like such a thing had never occurred to him.

"Keep your hands to yourself, simpleton," she said, and then we were moving again.

When we finally nudged and shoved our way up to the front of the ring, a man was already in there with Strangler. We tried to get Strangler's attention, but with the way the crowd was hooting and calling, our words got pushed down by the noise. We might as well have been using sign language.

The man in the ring was as big as Strangler, and younger. He came at Strangler, and Strangler jabbed him with a left, and the man went back a step. Strangler dove and grabbed the man's legs and hit him in the stomach with his head and took him down. When the man hit the mat, he hit so hard I was a little sick to my stomach. In the next moment, Strangler had the man by the ankle with both hands and had a leg thrown over the man's knee.

The man actually yelled "Uncle!"

Strangler let him go and stood up. The man got up. The referee took hold of Strangler's hand, preparing to raise it.

The man was supposed to be through, but he decided to throw a low blow at Strangler. The shot caught him in the groin. Strangler, unlike Timmy when Jane kicked him, took the blow and turned his head and looked at the man in a way that made me feel as if the world had just turned dark. Strangler jerked free of the ref, grabbed the man around the waist, and ran with him until he hit the ropes with the man's back.

He squeezed like he was trying to get grease out of a tube, and the man passed out.

Strangler just dropped him. A couple of men on the sidelines pulled the unconscious tough guy through the ropes and took him away.

Strangler called out, "Next."

We got on the steps that led up to the ring, hoping to get close enough to yell out to Strangler that the gangsters were there and looking for him, but the referee yelled for us to get down.

Strangler looked and saw us.

"They're here," I said, loud as I could.

Strangler let what I said hang in the air before he mouthed, "Don't matter."

Another man entered the ring, and Strangler went back to it. This guy was burly and only wearing pants and a T-shirt. He was a little bit more work for Strangler, but I think the truth was Strangler was giving the crowd a show. The last one had been too easy. The two of them flopped this way, and then they flopped the other way, and it all ended with the challenger pinned to the floor with Strangler's knee in his neck.

After three more challengers lost to Strangler, it was over. No one else wanted to step into the ring.

I looked this way and that for Bad Tiger and Timmy but didn't see them.

Strangler lifted up a ring rope and stepped under it onto the steps. As we backed down to let him pass, he picked up his sweatshirt. "You ought not to have come back with them around."

"You need to run," Jane said. "They were bound to find you, and now they have."

She pointed. Timmy was standing at the back of the crowd, which was beginning to break up.

"Me and him got to talk," Strangler said, and headed in that direction. But Timmy just turned and walked away briskly.

"I think he doesn't want to shoot you in this crowd," Jane said. "But I don't think he's giving up."

Strangler started across the lot carrying his sweatshirt. We followed.

"Go home, kids," he said.

"Ain't got no home," Tony said.

"Then go away."

"Why don't you run?" Jane said.

"'Cause I probably deserve what I'm going to get."

"Why? You gave the money back," she said.

We had crossed the lot now, and we could see Strangler's trailer. Bad Tiger was sitting on the steps smiling at us. I suppose we should have broke and ran right then, but we didn't. Like ducks, we followed Strangler to his trailer. Just before we got to the steps, Bad Tiger stood up, reached inside his coat, pulled out a gun, and held it to his side.

"Howdy, Strangler," Bad Tiger said.

"Just get it over with," Strangler said. "Kids ain't got nothing to do with it."

"Sure they do," said a voice behind us. "We're all old friends."

I turned and there was Timmy. He had his coat thrown back and his hand was across his chest, resting on the butt of his gun in its shoulder holster.

Timmy said, "I always wanted to try you, Strangler."

"No you don't," Strangler said. "You did, you wouldn't have your hand on that gun."

Timmy's face fell.

Bad Tiger turned and opened the door to Strangler's trailer, said, "Come on in. It's your place. You'll like it fine. For a moment."

Strangler went up the steps and inside, tossed the sweatshirt on the floor. We followed, Timmy behind us.

When we were in the trailer, Timmy shut the door.

The place was a wreck. Clothes thrown about, drawers open.

Bad Tiger said, "Cozy."

"I tell you, the kids ain't got nothing to do with nothing," Strangler said.

"Say they don't," Bad Tiger said. "They come to warn you. They did that, didn't they?"

"Yeah, what a coincidence," Timmy said. "Us here, and you three kiddies here. I'd call that a happy coincidence."

"You should have just gone on when I told you," Strangler said to us.

"You know," said Jane, "you're right."

"Yeah," Bad Tiger said, "when you're right, you're right. But, here's the thing, Strangler. We want the money."

"I haven't got it."

"The crippled kid?" Bad Tiger said. "Tell me, for your own sake, she's still crippled. That you didn't spend the money on that."

"There is no crippled kid."

Bad Tiger let that idea roam around inside his head.

"Saying you made that up?" Bad Tiger said.

"I just wanted to have a good reason to do something I shouldn't have. I was tired of this life. Then, after I done it, I thought this life wasn't so bad after all. I made that story up because I didn't want to just be a common thief, like you two. I mailed the money back."

Timmy laughed. It was the kind of laugh that was solid enough and sharp enough you could have whittled wood with it. "You are one big liar, Strangler," he said.

"Not about the money," he said.

Bad Tiger moved quickly and brought the gun barrel down on the side of Strangler's head. Strangler staggered back a step and turned his head sideways. When he looked back at Bad Tiger, there was blood running down the side of his face. He grinned. There was a look in his eyes akin to the look he gave the man that had hit him below the belt. I saw Bad Tiger's eyes shift a little when he saw that look. He didn't like it. He stepped back.

Strangler said, "My ole granny can hit harder than that, and she's got a bad arm."

"Yeah," Bad Tiger said, "well, let's see how a bullet in your gut goes. See how big a bite that is. No, tell you what. I'm going to start with the kids first. I'll take shorty there, and then you don't talk, I got to do one of the others. The girl, I'm going to shoot her several times. I really don't like her."

"Get in line," Jane said.

"You just don't learn, do you," Bad Tiger said. He raised the gun and pointed it at Jane.

Strangler said, "All right, now. I'll give you the money."

Everything went still and silent for a long moment.

"That's the way I figured," Timmy said. "I knew you had that money. Mailed it back, my butt."

"I got it, all right."

"So you didn't mail it back?" Jane said.

"No," Strangler said.

"Way you lie," Jane said, "you and me should team up."

Strangler laughed a little.

"Okay," Bad Tiger said. "You've had your chuckle, now show us the money."

Strangler moved over to a trunk on the floor and started to open it.

"Hold it," Bad Tiger said. "I done looked there. We threw this place earlier. If we found the money, we might have just left you."

"No we wouldn't have," Timmy said.

"You got to know where to look, and how," Strangler said.

"It could have been four ways," Bad Tiger said, "but you had to get cute. And Buddy, he had to get shot. You messed things up."

"Not for you two," Strangler said. "I give it to you now, you only have to split it two ways."

"Sure it's in there?" Timmy said.

"Yeah," Strangler said.

"All of you, get over there by the chest," Bad Tiger said.

"Yeah, that way, we start shooting, you'll be grouped up nice," Timmy said.

We went over and stood by the trunk, near Strangler.

204

Strangler opened the trunk and took out a small barbell and a few metal weights, placed them on the floor beside the trunk.

He turned and looked at Bad Tiger. "I'm going to have to have a pocketknife, something like that."

Bad Tiger reached his free hand into his pocket and took out a pocketknife and tossed it to Strangler. Strangler caught it, opened it. He bent down and reached into the trunk, caught the bottom edge with the knife, and wiggled the blade until the bottom came up.

It was a false bottom. The trunk was actually several inches deeper. There were bills in it. Lots of them. They were laid out in rows.

"I thought I was the liar," Jane said. "You got the touch. You told me your mama robbed the bank, not you, I might have believed you."

"I didn't spend a dollar," Strangler said.

Bad Tiger came closer and said to us, "While y'all are sorting your consciences, back over there a ways."

We moved. That put our backs against the wall.

"That's nice," Bad Tiger said, looking inside the trunk. "But is that all of it?"

"There's some in the bedroom," Strangler said.

"I looked in there," Bad Tiger said.

"You looked in here," Strangler said. "Now, split it up, shoot me, whatever, but let the kids go."

"Oh yeah," Bad Tiger said, turning slightly, looking at Timmy. "There ain't actually going to be no two-way split."

He shot Timmy in the chest. The sound of the shot in the

trailer made my ears ring like a telephone. Outside, though, with all the carnival racket going on, it wouldn't have sounded like much, if it was heard at all.

Timmy moved slightly but didn't drop. He just stood there. He looked at Bad Tiger like maybe it was all a joke. The bullet had gone right through him and slammed into the wall. He tried to shoot his gun, but it was suddenly too heavy for him to hold. It fell out of his hand and he went to one knee.

"For the record," Bad Tiger said, "I never liked you much."

Timmy leaned forward slightly, then fell on his face.

That's when it happened.

As Bad Tiger turned, Strangler, quick as a card cheat, dipped down and grabbed one of the weights and threw it, hit Bad Tiger in the face. Bad Tiger groaned and fell on his back. Strangler stepped forward and put his foot on Bad Tiger's gun hand. He pushed his weight down till Bad Tiger let go of the gun.

Bad Tiger made a noise like a rat trapped in a fruit jar, managed to jerk his hand free. As he got to his feet, Strangler hit him with a punch that knocked him across the room and into the front door.

The door wasn't closed so good, and when Bad Tiger flipped backwards against it, it flew open and he went tumbling down the stairs.

"Now I'm going to show you how you really hit someone," Strangler said, and picked up the little barbell.

By the time he started for the door, Bad Tiger was gone.

46

Outside, we saw Bad Tiger running across the lot in the direction of the rides. Strangler took off after him.

Jane said, "Well?"

She broke into a run, and we followed.

Darting between people and around concessions and booths, we followed Strangler and Bad Tiger to where the air was filled with the grinding and clanking of gears, shifting seats, and people yelling and laughing.

Bad Tiger was making good time, but Strangler, big man or not, was making better. We kept running after them, and then Bad Tiger came up against a swirling ride and stopped. The chairs with people in it swung down and back up, around and down again. Bad Tiger seemed kind of frozen by it. He looked at the ride; then he turned and looked at us. But mainly he looked at Strangler and that barbell.

Bad Tiger reached down and pulled up his pants cuff. There was a little holster there, and in the little holster was a little revolver.

Like I said, it wasn't a big gun, but any gun if it's pointed at you is big, which is why little men love to carry them.

He pointed it at Strangler.

"I ain't running no more," Bad Tiger said.

"You've run all your life," Strangler said. "You ain't nothing but a runner."

"Yeah, you think so. I tell you, I ain't running from you no more. You best just let me go."

"Without your money." The way Strangler said it, I thought he was about to break out and snicker.

"I don't need no money. Banks got plenty of money."

"Nah," Strangler said. "I let you go, I figure I'm going to have to see you again, and I don't want to."

Strangler advanced with the barbell.

"Then I'll shoot you."

"I just don't care," Strangler said, and stepped forward.

Bad Tiger fired the gun.

47

The bullet hit Strangler, I knew that, but all he did was grunt and shift a bit, and then he was walking again. Blood was running down his side. His mouth was twisted up and there was spittle on his lips.

Bad Tiger looked at Strangler like he'd just discovered that a martian had landed at the carnival. He was so startled, he backed up a step.

He fired again.

This time I heard the bullet slam into something behind us. I turned my head and saw one of the teddy bears at a booth topple over, bleeding white cotton stuffing.

Strangler was less than three feet away from Bad Tiger now. He made a noise in his throat like a dog growling over a bone. People had started to understand what was happening. A lady screamed. There were yells from the spinning ride. The guy that worked the ride lever said, "Hey now, hey now," and he made a quick retreat around the other side of the ride. I hoped he was going to get some law.

Bad Tiger yelled and pulled the trigger.

The gun barked.

Strangler staggered, but he still didn't go down.

Bad Tiger took one more step back, and that was when it happened.

He stepped right in between the whirling seats of a ride, but he was there for less than the blink of an eye. The next seat swinging around caught him solid, and I got to tell you, it was an amazing and a horrible sight.

It lifted him so quick it was hard to believe it was happening. It was like he had learned to fly.

He was tossed like a Raggedy Ann doll. It flung him up, and he fell back down. But he didn't hit the ground. He was struck again by another seat and bounced into a pole. That bounced him back into another spinning seat, and that one caught him in such a way that he was knocked across the lot at a height of about thirty feet. He went like he had been shot out of a cannon.

We watched with amazement as he crashed into a popcorn stand and it exploded in a rain of white puffy corn and a running man. Oily butter leaked yellow over the ground. Bad Tiger's suit soaked it up like a fresh biscuit.

Bad Tiger didn't move. He was facedown and one arm was twisted behind his back like he was trying to scratch a hard-to-reach spot low down.

"Oh," Tony said. "Oh my."

"Yeah," I said. "Oh my."

Dazed, we walked over to Strangler. He was holding his hand against his left side. There was a bloody spot on the right side of his bare chest as well. But Strangler, he was still standing.

A crowd gathered around Bad Tiger, but then they just

stood there looking at him. One man stepped forward and nudged Bad Tiger's body with the toe of his shoe, like he was trying to wake him up.

Someone else yelled, "Get a doctor!"

Strangler said, "I can tell you from here. Ain't no need to check his pulse."

48

A while later an ambulance sped up with its siren on and two men jumped out and opened the back and rolled out a stretcher, headed for where Bad Tiger lay.

They picked him up and turned him over gently, put him on the stretcher. One of the men carrying him, said, "Well, he's ate his last pickle."

A man in the crowd pointed at Strangler.

"He was shooting at that guy, the one without a shirt, and he backed into the ride while he was doing it."

"Not our department," said one of the ambulance men.

They put him in the ambulance and drove away. No siren, moving slowly. No one in a hurry now.

We walked with Strangler to his trailer. Inside, he put the false bottom in the trunk, replaced the barbells and all the rest back inside, and closed the lid. He sat on the couch and looked at Timmy. Timmy looked smaller than I remembered.

After a while, the cops came, two of them. They knocked on the door politely, and when I let them in they looked at the body on the floor, then at us. One of the cops was thin with a sweet face. The other was a stocky cop who looked like he ate bullets for breakfast and cannons for dinner. For supper, maybe the cannonballs.

Jane was wrapping Strangler's side. There was already a bandage on his chest.

She said, "I reckon both bullets are still in him."

"He looks spry for two bullets," said the stocky cop.

"Yeah, well," Jane said, "he is naturally spry."

The cops walked over and looked at Strangler.

"Someone called a doctor," said the thin cop. "He's on his way."

"I'm all right," Strangler said. "It wasn't much of a gun."

"You could still use a doctor, " Jane said.

"You know," said the stocky cop, "we got a body on the floor, we got another one thrown through a popcorn stand, twisted up like a Boy Scout knot, but we ain't got no explanation."

"He tried to rob Strangler," Jane said.

"Who are you?" the cop said.

"A fan. I run his fan club. He doesn't know it yet, but we just started one. We came here to tell him that, and that's how we got mixed up in all this mess. We're from Oklahoma."

"Oklahoma?" the stocky cop said.

"Yeah, state just above Texas," Jane said.

The thin cop grinned. The stocky cop said, "Yeah, girlie, I know where it is. But why did you come all the way from Oklahoma?"

"We are all fans of Strangler," she said. "Right?"

She looked at us when she said that.

Tony nodded.

I nodded.

"Fans?" said the stout cop.

"Big fans," Jane said.

"So you heard of Strangler here, and you come all the way down from Oklahoma to tell him you're starting a fan club?"

"Well," Jane said, resting a hand on Strangler's shoulder, "it's a little more complicated than that. We didn't like the weather, the drought, the sand, the grasshoppers, the starving rabbits, the centipedes everywhere, the scorpions, and did I mention the dust?"

"You did," said the stocky cop. "You're a little smarty, ain't you?"

"I like to think so," Jane said.

"That's not what I meant," said the cop.

"All I'm saying, sir, is we've had a hard time, and we were very excited to be here, to finally tell our hero about the fan club. And frankly, we were looking for a job with the carnival. Strangler has quite a following in Oklahoma and the South. East Texas especially. We thought a fan club would be nice. And we thought a quarter per membership could add up."

"So it was a way to make money?" said the thin cop.

"Money," Jane said, "and a way to honor our hero. We just came to tell him. We wanted his blessing. Course, I'll be honest with you. With or without it, we were going to form the fan club anyway."

"So, fan club aside," said the stocky cop. "How'd all this happen?"

"Simple," Jane said.

"Don't you talk?" the stocky cop said to Strangler.

"Yeah, but she's explaining real good," Strangler said.

"As fate would have it," Jane said, "we tracked Strangler down, came by to tell him about our plans, and those two dreadful men, they tried to rob him. The man that crashed the popcorn stand, he shot that man on the floor there over some argument. We don't even really understand what he was mad about, do we?"

This was directed at all of us.

Tony shook his head.

I shook mine.

Strangler said, "Yeah, it was kind of confusing."

"My take," Jane said, "if you want it, is they come to rob poor Strangler here, they didn't want to share it with one another. You know the story. No honor among thieves. My guess is they were already feuding over something and it got carried into their work, so to speak. It came to a head right here."

"Why would they want to rob you any more than anyone else here?"

"I don't know," Strangler said. "I don't have anything."

"He's famous," Jane said. "Fame draws good and it draws bad. They were bad."

"I'll say," said the cop.

"They thought he had money," Jane said. "Just because he's a famous fighter, they thought he had some real dough. But, alas. He does most of what he does for the love of it. Right, Strangler?"

"Right," Strangler said.

"For the love of it, huh?" said the stocky cop.

"You know who that was?" said the thin cop. "The one that ate the popcorn stand? That was Bad Tiger."

"The gangster?" Jane said. "Oh my. And who's that on the floor, Dillinger?"

"Timmy Durango," said the stocky cop. "He goes by other names, but that's his real one. He's bad as any of them. It was Bad Tiger, though, that was the brains."

"He ain't got any now," said the thin cop, "unless you want to gather them up and put them in a popcorn bag."

"Crime doesn't pay," Jane said. "And that's just the long and the short of the matter, don't you think?"

"You really do talk a lot," the stocky cop said to Jane.

"It's a gift," she said.

49

We spent some time down at the station while Strangler was with the doctor getting the bullets pulled out, and we all told the story Jane told. It wasn't that good a story, but it was as good as any other. No one even thought Strangler might have ever robbed a bank. And if they thought there was any stinky fish in our story, they didn't say so, least not direct-like.

When it was over, the cops drove us back to Strangler's trailer, which was the only place we had to stay, and we took a nap. Tony on the couch, me and Jane sleeping in chairs. When we woke up, Strangler still wasn't home, but we were hungry.

We found some bread and canned goods and made sandwiches, and were eating when Strangler came in. He was dressed in a loose shirt and dress pants and regular shoes. They were the clothes he took with him when the police hauled us off.

I felt kind of funny, us eating his food and him standing

216

there in the doorway. Jane, however, seemed quite comfortable.

Jane said, "Can I fix you something?"

"I'm all right," he said. "That was some lie you told," he said to Jane.

"It's her specialty," I said.

"I just felt the truth lacked something," she said.

"They believed it good enough," he said. "They're just happy to have public enemies off the charts. Those two had let me go and gone on about their business, they'd be alive today. Well, Bad Tiger might be. I think he was planning to shoot Timmy all along."

"About the money, Strangler," Jane said.

"I know. I lied to everyone, then lied to myself, but it's something to have a liar like you call me on lying."

"Mine doesn't hurt anyone," she said. "It helped."

"This time," I said.

"All right, this time," Jane said. "But you got all that money, and that's the bank's money."

"Banks aren't people," Strangler said.

"Sure they are," Jane said. "Who do you think puts money in the bank?"

Strangler went over and sat on the trunk with the money. He said, "Yeah. I know. I know good. I really did intend to send it back. I mean, I do intend to send it back. I kept it to look at for a while. To think about what I might have done had I kept it."

"You might have spent about ten years in jail," Jane said. "You still might."

"You'd say something about it?" Strangler said.

"I don't know," Jane said.

"Me either," I said.

"I wouldn't tell," Tony said. "Me, I don't care. I could use some money."

I could tell that sort of hit Strangler where he lived.

"Nah, you ain't that way," Strangler said to Tony. "You and me, we ain't like that. I made a mistake, but I got to make it right."

"Don't make it so right you go to jail," I said.

"I'm not wanting to make it that right," he said. "Tomorrow, I get some boxes, and you kids help me mail it back. That all right?"

"I suggest we drive someplace not so close to mail it," Jane said. "They might trace it somehow, and if they see it come from around here, and they get to thinking about Bad Tiger and Timmy looking you up, it could all come together, and not in a good way."

"I suppose you're right," Strangler said.

"We can pack boxes with the money," Jane said, "and we can make a note with words cut from newspapers and glue them on paper. We can put the note inside one of the boxes with the money. It can say something like: *Here's the money back, sorry.* No signature, of course"

"That sounds good," Strangler said.

"We can drive to someplace in Louisiana to mail it," Jane said.

So that was the plan, and that's what we did. After that, well, there's not much left to tell.

218

We stayed at Strangler's trailer for a while, because none of us had any real place to go, except Tony. I guess Jane and I were welcome at Mrs. Carson's, but, truth be told, we'd tasted too much of the world and had adventures, and we weren't ready to settle down.

Me and Jane took a day and drove over to the Winona area in Junior's truck. I wanted to give it back, and we'd also get to see Gasper. I hoped Junior would drive us back to the carnival after.

I found the road where Junior lived, and we drove down there. The house was empty. It looked as if no one had ever lived there. There was no note. Junior and Gasper and Nasty were gone. I know it's not very satisfactory, but that's how the truth is sometimes, because we never saw or heard from them again. I like to think they went up north for work and found it. Nasty being the exception. I just hoped he had a warm fire to lie in front of.

As for the truck, well, Junior said he didn't care if he got it back, and now I knew he meant it.

We drove back to the carnival, and for the next few days we taught Jane how to drive. She took to it like a squirrel to hickory nuts. It wasn't no time at all till she could keep the car on the right side of the road and could steer with one hand and wave to folks with the other. Strangler said she was a natural. Fact is, she was a dang site better than me in two days. I didn't like hearing that, but it was the truth. Tony decided he wanted to go back to Mrs. Carson. Me and Jane didn't like the idea on one hand, but we figured it was for the best. He liked having a home, and ought to have one.

Besides, growing up with either of us, me and Jane decided, was akin to being raised by wolves.

Jane had a few dollars, and Strangler gave Tony a few, and she and Tony left early one morning.

It all happened so fast the day they left, I didn't feel I got to tell either one of them a proper goodbye.

Jane said she'd write in care of the carnival, general delivery. The carnival's next town was Tyler, so she said she'd send it there. She did just that, and the letter said she was coming to see me.

She came and I met her in Tyler, at the carnival. Me and her and Strangler had a visit, and then later that night I walked with her off the carnival lot and we rode in Junior's truck, which was now her truck, and we ended up at a spot outside of town where the earth rose up high and there were lots of trees and a little drop-off where you could see the dark roll of a few hills and the high bright light of the moon and the stars.

She sat with her hands on the wheel. She said, "Sometimes I lie a little."

"I know that."

"I love Tony, and I want him to be happy," she said. "I even dragged him all over creation with us. But that isn't what he wants, Jack."

"I know that too."

"He's happy where he is. I'm not."

Suddenly, my stomach felt a little queasy. "I was planning on getting loose from the carnival, coming to see you and Tony."

220

"You love the carnival. I can tell."

This was true, but I didn't say anything.

"I think a person ought to go their own way, if that way is tugging at them," she said. "You know what I mean?"

"I think so. But I don't know it bodes well for me."

"Let's don't talk about it anymore. Kiss me, Jack."

I did. Long and hard. It was as sweet a kiss as I ever had. When it was finished, Jane leaned forward and cranked the truck. The moonlight was bright enough I could see tears on her cheeks.

We drove out of there then, back to the carnival, but when we got there, Jane didn't get out. She said, "I got a long ways to go, so I'm going to get after it."

"Tonight?"

"Tony will expect me back."

"All right," I said.

She leaned over and kissed me on the mouth. Kissed me good. I gave her the same kind of kiss, and feeling a little stunned, I got out of the truck.

"Goodbye," she said as I held the door.

"Goodbye," I said. "I love you."

I hadn't planned it, but the words had just jumped out of my mouth like a frightened frog.

She smiled at me. "I'll write."

"I'll be in Hawkins in a few days," I said. "Send it to general delivery there. I'll leave a follow-up address for when we move on."

"That's good," she said.

Without really thinking about it, I gently closed the door,

then watched as the truck moved away, rattling along, picking up speed, heading down the road, into the moonlight.

50

She didn't write.

A few days later, I rode with Strangler to Hawkins, and pretty soon I was helping out with the carnival. Helping Strangler, actually. Kind of an assistant. He paid me for the work. It wasn't much, but it was money, and it was my own money. I was a carny and I loved it.

Thing is, though, we got to Hawkins, and I went to the little post office there every day, and no letter ever came.

I had Mrs. Carson's address, and I wrote Jane when we moved on to Texarkana. I told her to address my mail to the Memphis post office, general delivery. That was our next stop.

When we got to Memphis there was a letter for me from Mrs. Carson. She wrote that Jane had moved on. I felt like my insides had fallen out of me.

Moved on?

That wasn't quite what I had hoped for.

The carnival wound up into Missouri and even Kentucky, before coming back down along the edge of Oklahoma. When we got there, Strangler bought a car, and he let me borrow it. It was an older car, but it ran fine. I drove on across Oklahoma to where Mrs. Carson lived.

It was a pretty burnt-out state, the dust still blowing, the grasshoppers still eating. I had a little money saved up now, so I stopped and got gas and ate at cafés, and even stayed a night in a boardinghouse. All things considered, it was a pretty comfortable trip compared with the one I had taken with Jane and Tony.

But, I got to be honest, it wasn't as much fun.

When I got to Mrs. Carson's, I went up to the house and knocked, and she was glad to see me, and Tony was too. He told me he had been going to school, and he loved it, and had only been in two fights.

I thought that was pretty good.

Jane didn't write them often, Mrs. Carson said, but the last time she had written, she had sent a letter for me. She said Jane wrote in their letter she figured I'd show up there eventually, and would they give it to me.

I didn't open it right away. I ate supper with Mrs. Carson and Tony, and then I had coffee with some pie, and Tony had milk and a lot of pie, and then me and him went out on the porch swing and sat there in the soft night watching the fireflies flit about.

Tony said, "I miss Jane, but I got to say, Jack, I like it here."

223

"Mrs. Carson is a good woman."

"She's like a mother, I think. I didn't really have one that mattered, so I don't know what one is supposed to be like. My mother is out there somewhere with a Bible salesman. But Mrs. Carson, she seems to like me."

"Sure she does."

"She said she's going to adopt me."

"I'm glad you're happy," I said.

"Yeah, but you don't look so happy," he said.

"I guess I miss Jane too," I said.

"She liked you," Tony said.

"Not enough," I said.

"It's just the spirit in her," Tony said. "She's got lots of spirit. You can't hold that spirit down. It was hard for her to leave me. She tried to explain it to me, but she couldn't. But she didn't need to. I knew she had to leave. I don't like it, but I knew it was coming."

I smiled at him. "You've grown up a lot in a short time," I said.

"You think?" he said.

"I think."

51

I spent the night there, and Mrs. Carson put me in the room I was in before. Tony had his own room now, so it was just me in there.

I turned on the lamp by the bed and sat down on the edge and opened the letter.

I unfolded it and read:

> Dear Jack,
>
> I know I hurt your feelings, because I know you wanted more from me, and if I was going to be special with anyone, you'd be the one.
>
> But I am not ready for that. I know my nature. I figured I should just cut the rope quick, not because I don't care about you, but because I got to see the world and what's out there. Just not ready to settle down and sew and cook and have babies. Though I would like a dog.
>
> Now, I know you're going to think this is a lie, 'cause I

been known to lie, but I have gone off to California. I've got me a big notebook and a bunch of pencils and a pocketknife to keep them sharp, and I'm writing about what I see.

I'm writing about these folks that want to create unions. I'm writing about trains and hoboes. I've got real good at riding trains.

I want to learn to fly a plane.

I want to learn to sail a boat.

I plan to write a book.

Maybe I'll see you someday. Maybe you and me will have a laugh, or another kiss.

By the way, I really liked that kiss.

May you have what you want in life. I hope the same for Tony. And I hope the same for me.

Love, Jane

I didn't know exactly what to make of it, but that's all there was. Next day I got in Strangler's car and caught up with the carnival. It had gone across the Red River and was in northern Texas, at a place called Paris.

It wasn't much like I pictured Paris to be. I had always thought it would be like Texas's answer to the one in France. But it was just a hot little town where people came to the carnival, and Strangler won every bout.

I don't know if I'll stay with the carnival or not. I sure like Strangler, and I like the job of making him run and work out and eat right. I like making sure he's ready for his bouts, and I manage his side bets. He makes quite a few, and he always wins. But I don't know if I'll stay. I don't know if it's enough, and it darn sure can't last forever. Strangler is no spring chicken.

"Someday," he told me, "when I feel one of them younger ones is making it too hard for me, I'm going to retire and go into another line of work."

"What will that be, Strangler?" I asked.

"Brain surgeon," he said, and laughed.

So, here I am, Strangler in his bedroom asleep, and me about to lie down on my couch. But before I do that, I thought I'd sit here with the lamp on, a writing pad on the table, and a sharp pencil in my hand, so I can put all the things down on paper that happened to us.

Guess I got that idea from Jane.

I hope she's doing well.

I hope she's finding what she wants out there.

I know I'll never forget her. I love her, but truth to tell, I don't know a whole lot about love. It confuses me. So maybe Jane was right to not let that go too far. Not with us as young as we are, with so much future stretched out in front of us.

But sometimes, right before I fall asleep, I think I can taste her lips, and they are sweet.

She was an awful liar, but still, she was so smart and so beautiful. She sure was something.

all the earth, thrown to the sky

joe r. lansdale

A READER'S GUIDE

discussion starters

1. Discuss the meaning of the title.

2. Jack's mother tells him that if you look hard, you can "see the face of the devil" (p. 1) in the sandstorms. When does Jack first "see the face of the devil" in the sand?

3. Why does Jack feel that his father has taken the coward's way out? Jack says, "I hadn't never been no coward and wasn't about to start" (p. 3). Discuss the differences between cowardice and courage. What is Jack's first act of courage in the novel? How does Jane help him when his courage is tested?

4. Abandonment is a central theme of the novel. How does the Dust Bowl setting enhance this theme? Compare the ways in which Jack, Jane, and Tony have been abandoned, and discuss how each deals with his or her situation. Name other characters in the novel who are abandoned. Does Jack feel abandoned by Jane at the end of the novel?

5. How is Jack's idea of family different from Jane's? Why does Jack say that his daddy could have loved him more? Discuss the ways in which Jack, Jane, and Tony become a family as they make their way to Texas. Why is Tony so loyal to Jane? Why does he decide to live with Mrs. Carson?

6. Jack has suspicions early on that Jane is a "born liar" (p. 31). Why is he so willing to accept her lies? How does her skill at lying both help and hinder them on their journey? Is she lying or simply stretching the truth for the sake of survival? Why does Jane believe Strangler's story? Why does Jack feel guilty for "hoodwinking" Mrs. Carson?

7. Lying is difficult for Jack, but stealing is even harder. How does he justify taking Old Man Turpin's car? The kids come face to face with evil when they meet Bad Tiger, Timmy, and Buddy. Discuss their reactions when they witness Timmy killing Buddy.

8. Explain what Jack means when he says that he doesn't feel good about himself now that he's on the run with "real gangsters." Describe Strangler's character. How does he defend his crime? Discuss the kids' reaction when they discover that Strangler is lying.

9. The kids get into several life-threatening predicaments. How does Jane's strength keep them hopeful that they can escape the jams they are in?

10. Jane says that she and Jack are good judges of character. Do you think she's right? Who is the better judge of character, Jack or Jane?

11. Jane thinks that a "quest" will tell them who they really are. Discuss the differences between an adventure and a quest. At what point does their adventure become a quest? Why is having a quest so important to Jane?

12. Jane says, "I want to do something that gives me adventure and does something noble for someone" (p. 92). Do you think she achieves her goal? What are her noble acts? She accuses Jack of being "easily satisfied" (p. 92). How are Jack and Jane's differences reflected in their decisions at the end of the novel?

13. Jack decides to work at the carnival with Strangler for the foreseeable future but says, "I don't know if I'll stay. I don't know if it's enough" (p. 227). What type of life would be "enough" for Jack?

14. At the beginning of the novel, Jack says that he would like to be a hero. Does he achieve his goal?

Author Q & A

A CONVERSATION WITH
JOE R. LANSDALE

Q: How is writing for kids different from writing for adults?

A: Frankly, it isn't as different as it was thirty or forty years ago, certainly not as much as when I was a kid. Books were then easily divided. In this day and time kids grow up quicker, or at least they are more knowledgeable at an early age. Almost any subject that fits adults fits young adults. There are exceptions, but the bottom line is a good story is a good story, and if you have a story to tell, a good YA should also appeal to adults.

Q: You are an accomplished writer of fantasy and mystery. How did you decide to write a historical adventure novel for kids?

A: Actually, I've written historicals before. I've always loved them. My novels *The Bottoms*, *A Fine Dark Line*, *Edge of Dark Water*, and *The Boar* all have young adult narrators, and all are coming-of-age novels, same as *All the Earth, Thrown to the Sky*. The adult novels are a little harsher in their design, but thematically, they are similar to this book. All take place in the thirties, except *A Fine Dark Line*, which takes place in the fifties. *The Magic Wagon* has a young protagonist and could easily have been published as a YA novel. I read a lot of YA literature, so I think I know the field pretty well, but I'm not driven by what's popular as much as I am driven by what I want to write. That's not as popular with publishers, by the way, and I understand their concerns, but I also understand my own.

Q: Which genre do you enjoy writing the most?

A: There isn't any one genre I prefer. I like all the genres I've written in, but I don't think of myself as someone who chases genre. The only genre I care about is the Lansdale genre. By the time you chase down the next trend, so have a lot of others, and when you look up, it's gone, or you're just another one in a long line of soon-to-be forgotten books. There are exceptions, but I see that all the time. I may end up writing something in a popular trend, but if I do, it will be because I want to, because that is what's driving me. I'll go where my excitement leads me. As a writer, to do otherwise leads to boredom, and if you bore yourself, you bore the reader. What I mostly like are novels about people and how they react to dire circumstances. I probably write a lot about the Great Depression because my parents lived through it and I grew up with their stories.

Q: The Dust Bowl era and the Great Depression were tough times in America. What research did you do for *All the Earth, Thrown to the Sky*? Did you use primary documents and oral histories?

A: As I said, my parents told me stories about it all my life. They were in their twenties when the Great Depression hit. They had grown up poor, but the Depression was an incredibly sad and anxious time. I have read about it all my life, and a lot of the novels I enjoy reading were written during that time, so I have a pretty good feel for the era. That's not to say I didn't make some mistakes. I may have. Probably did. But I tried to stay as true to the era as I could. So I used oral histories and documents, but I didn't know I was researching at the time. I was listening and reading because it fascinated me.

Q: Will you make a statement to young readers about the importance of reading historical fiction?

A: They say we can learn not to make the same mistakes by reading about the past. Unfortunately, that isn't always true. We do seem to make a lot of the same mistakes, but many can be prevented. We can also learn that others have lived through what we are living through, good and bad, and that there is a continuation of human spirit from one generation to the next. And it's always fascinating to see how people lived without the things we now take for granted every day. History is a long line of human mistakes and triumphs. We need to know its different sides; understanding the many sides of our character and our human journey is essential to knowing who we are as individuals.

Q: What is your writing process? Did you know how this novel would end when you began writing it?

A: I never know how one of my novels will end while I'm writing. I find a mood, sort of like a piece of music I hear and can't identify. I sit down and start writing. I write a little each morning, and then the next morning I start over. One day I look up and I have a novel, or story, or screenplay, or comic script.

Q: There are many themes in the novel: abandonment, family, survival, and hope. How do you think these themes apply to kids' lives today?

A: People are people, then and now. The same sorts of trials and tribulations face us from one generation to the next. The exact nature of these challenges may change, but they are still going to

11

confront us. And many of them never change. Every generation must decide who they are and what they plan to do with their lives. In some ways we all experience abandonment, family, survival, and hope, but how we face them is what matters. We are either people with character or people without it.

Q: Which character in the novel do you most admire?

A: I love all the main characters. I think I'm a bit of all of them. Jane and Jack are certainly my two sides: the adventurous one, and the one that just wants a steady life and a good home.

Q: What do you read for pleasure?

A: I read all manner of books and stories. I read science fiction. Classic literature. Crime. Horror. Mystery. I read for good writing and good characters and good stories. That's all I need to find a book interesting. As for the writers I read, they are too varied to list here, but some I've enjoyed are Gary Paulson, Ray Bradbury, Raymond Chandler, John Steinbeck, Andrew Vachss, and Flannery O'Connor. My favorite novel is *To Kill a Mockingbird*. Anyway, this list could go on and on, so I'll stop here.

Q: What are some of the questions you get from young readers?

A: You've asked them. They don't always state them in the way they are presented here, but these are the kinds of things they ask. What I sometimes get from adults is that my young characters seem too wise and too smart. This only leads me to conclude that they don't know many young people as well as they think.

JOE R. LANSDALE is the author of more than a dozen novels for adults, including eight Hap and Leonard novels, as well as *Sunset and Sawdust* and *Lost Echoes*. He has received a British Fantasy Award, an American Mystery Award, an Edgar Award, a Grinzane Cavour Prize, and nine Bram Stoker Awards. He lives with his family in Nacogdoches, Texas.

Jack Catcher's parents are dead—his mom died of a sickness and his dad of a broken heart—and he wants to get out of Oklahoma, where dust storms have killed everything green and hopeful. So when former classmate Jane Lewis and her little brother, Tony, show up in his yard with plans to steal a dead neighbor's car and make a break for Texas, Jack doesn't need much convincing to go with them. But a run-in with one of the era's most notorious gangsters puts a crimp in Jane's plan, and soon the three orphans are riding the rails among hoboes, gangsters, and con men, racing to warn a carnival-wrestler-turned-bank-robber of the danger headed toward him faster than a black blizzard on the prairie horizon.

All the Earth, Thrown to the Sky is a thrilling road-trip adventure through the 1930s Dust Bowl of the Great Depression, when home was anywhere you hung your hat and family was often whoever sat around your campfire.

US $7.99 / $8.99 CAN

ISBN 978-0-385-73932-0

50799

9 780385 739320

randomhouse.com/teens

EMBER

Cover art © 2011 by Emmanuelle Brisson/Getty Images
Cover design by Kenny Holcomb